Cherokee Summer

Cherokee Summer

Glenn R. Parsons

CHEROKEE SUMMER
Youthful Misadventures in Rural Alabama
Glenn R. Parsons

DEDICATIONS

I dedicate this book to the following:

Thomas E. Parsons

A World War II veteran of the South Pacific, a wonderful storyteller, and the greatest father a kid could have.

Cheryl B. Parsons

My loving wife for her patience.

Erin Parsons Garrett

My beautiful daughter.

Tanner (T.J.) Parsons

My wonderful son.

SYNOPSIS

Set in 1960s Alabama, two young boys learn the ways of nature after they are befriended by an elderly Native American. Through various misadventures, the youngster's bond with the last Cherokee in north Alabama. After a summer of giant catfish, Native American ceremony, and unforgettable characters, the boys make a solemn vow that sends them across rural Alabama towards an unknown fate.

PRAISE FOR CHEROKEE SUMMER:
"Fast-paced and fun!"
"A thoroughly enjoyable read!"
"Characters vividly created!"
"Wonderfully insightful and funny!"
"A feel-good read!"
"An ending that will leave you spellbound!
"A cross between 'A Christmas Story and 'Stand by Me!"

FORWARD
I wrote this book with the intention of making it appropriate for the 14 to adult age group. Although a little crude in places, I believe I have accomplished this. There is no inappropriate language, no graphic violence, and no adult situations. I have depicted some characters in dramatic, "real-world" situations, but none of these will the reader find offensive. If they do, I will apologize now. I believe there are some important life lessons presented regarding respect, dignity, and faith. Many of the events and characters that are described in this novel were adapted from stories told to me by my father Thomas E. Parsons; others happened to me during my childhood growing up in Hueytown, Alabama, and still others are purely fictional. I genuinely hope you enjoy this little story.

Other Books by Glenn R. Parsons

Sharks, Skates, and Rays of the Gulf of Mexico: A Field Guide. Published by University Press of Mississippi, Jackson, MS. A field guide covering the habits, biology, and identification of sharks, skates and rays from Gulf of Mexico waters.

Introductory Fish Biology: An Ecophysiological Approach. Published by Cambridge Scholars Publishing, Cambridge, U.K. In-depth coverage of general fish biology focusing principally on the interface between fish biology and the environment.

Night Fishing. A new novel by Glenn R. Parsons. An excerpt: *The tiger shark had followed the boat for several hours, attracted first by the low-frequency sounds that a working shrimp boat created and further reinforced by the smell of dead and dying fish that trailed behind. A twelve-foot female, her sensory systems fired urgent signals into her walnut-sized brain, alerting her that food was nearby. Having found no prey in days, she was very hungry and the 38 "pups" she carried in her swollen belly were even hungrier. The crew working on the deck of the shrimp boat, Crimson Tide, was well aware that on most nights, the darkened waters around the fishing vessel teemed with large, hungry sharks as the boat crawled along at no more than a couple of knots.*

ABOUT THE AUTHOR

Glenn R. Parsons is a graduate of The University of Alabama, Birmingham, The University of South Alabama, Mobile, and he holds a PhD in Biological Oceanography from The School of Marine Science at the University of South Florida, St. Petersburg. He is Professor Emeritus and Past Director of the Center for Biodiversity and Conservation Research at Ole Miss. He lives in Oxford, Mississippi, with his wife, where he enjoys fishing the freshwaters of Mississippi and the coastal waters of the Gulf of America, hunting but rarely killing anything, reading, working on his 1962 Ford Fairlane 500, and riding his motorcycle. However, his greatest joy comes from writing, playing guitar, and spending time with his family, especially his two rambunctious grandsons. He can be reached at: glennp1776@gmail.com, and your comments and questions are welcome. He especially welcomes hearing from young readers who might be interested in a career in biology or marine biology.

The small open boat was entirely too far out in the main stream of the swirling Black Warrior River. Its passengers, two young boys, could clearly hear the low thrumming of diesel engines, but the fog and the wind made it almost impossible to determine the direction from which the sound was coming. Indeed, the sound seemed to be all around them and getting louder. The boys were on the verge of panic. Furiously paddling, they had no idea that they were heading directly into the path of a 200-ton tugboat.

Captain Tom Wells, at the wheel of the tugboat "Crimson Tide", peered into the foggy night as he steered the huge vessel downstream, trying to avoid the snags and continuously shifting sandbars of the Black Warrior. This stretch of the river was particularly treacherous. Although there was a full moon, the heavy fog and ominous dark clouds that scudded across the night sky made navigation extremely tricky. From time to time, just to ease his rattled nerves, he would turn on the large search light that was mounted on the wheelhouse and scan the river and bank. Tom pulled his pouch of Red Man from his back pocket and stuffed a large wad of pungent chewing tobacco into his cheek.

Captain Tom was descended from a long line of boat captains. His great-grandfather had piloted the Southern Belle, a Mississippi River steamboat that ran between Cairo, Illinois and New Orleans, Louisiana. On a trip back from New Orleans, The Belle caught fire at the mouth of Horn Lake, Tennessee. Fire on a ship is one of the worst things that can happen, and quick thinking is the only thing that can save you. Immediately turning the steamer into the lake, he ran it aground in shallow water near the lake shore. Unfortunately, the ship was quickly consumed by flames and was a total loss. The two smokestacks remained visible above the water's surface like limbless trees for 50 years afterwards.

Tom leaned out of the wheelhouse door into the damp night air and spat a long brown stream of tobacco juice into the Warrior. As he pulled his head back into the wheelhouse, he thought he caught a glimpse of something in the water just ahead of the vessel. He squinted hard, trying to decide if his mind and the river were playing tricks on him because there appeared to be something dead ahead. Tom quickly grabbed the control arm of the search light, flipped it on, and aimed it ahead of the vessel. There, to his horror, was a small boat not 20 feet off his bow. Two young boys, startled by the brilliant light, simultaneously turned to look in the direction of the approaching boat. Tom grabbed the wheel of the tugboat and frantically spun it to port in a futile attempt to avoid certain collision. At the same time, he throttled back on the engines and threw the vessel into reverse.

In the glaring spotlight, the unfolding tragedy seemed surreal. The huge bow of the tug hit the small boat mid-ship. The sound of breaking wood and screaming was gut-wrenching as the force of the huge bow of the tug drove the boat and both occupants down into the murky depths. The small boat was reduced to splinters as the two young boys were tossed like rag dolls into the cold river. Operating only on reflex, Tom threw the engine into neutral and dove into the Warrior, leaving the Crimson Tide adrift. As he entered the water, his elbow brushed against an object. Tom grabbed the sleeveless arm and kicked to the surface. But even before he could reach the bank of the river, his worst fears were confirmed. Swimming as hard as he could, Tom managed to get to the shore. He pulled one lifeless body onto the muddy bank of the Warrior. He knew his chance of finding the other was not good.

C hapter 1.

I first met Jack Feather at Howton's Fishing Camp on the banks of the Warrior River in northeast Alabama. I was fishing, he was running his dogs on a late spring day, sun low in a clear blue sky. Jack's appearance was unlike any I had ever seen. The first thing I noticed about him was his hair; snow white, cascading in a ponytail down the middle of his back. He was short, heavy-set, slightly bent, with a hawk-like nose and skin like ancient leather, cracked and creviced from his 73 hot Alabama summers and frigid winters. Jack was the only Cherokee I ever knew.

"Having any luck?" asked Jack as he approached.

"Not much." I was sitting on a log at the water's edge with my fishing pole in hand. I was not sure that I should be talking to this stranger.

"You catfish fishing?" asked Jack.

"Yeah, but right now I'll take anything."

"What you using for bait?"

"Worms."

"There are some good fish around here. Fish large enough to break that fishing pole like a toothpick."

"Yeah, I know." I was tempted to mention the big flathead catfish I had caught two summers ago, but decided against it.

"BEAU... BEAU! Get the heck away from there." One of Jack's dogs, a big yellow cur, had found a rotted fish on the riverbank and was lying on his back, wallowing around on it.

"That stupid dog loves to wallow in the gosh-awful, smelliest mess it can find," said Jack, "and I gotta put him in the car with me to get him home."

"I wonder why they do that?"

"Dogs do that to hide their scent. If they can cover up their own smell, they can sneak up on animals. It makes them better hunters. Of course, dogs don't hunt much anymore, except for their chew bones, but they still have a lot of wolf in them."

"You know I never really thought about it, but that makes sense."

"Yes, it makes a lot of very stinky sense," said Jack, laughing. "That's a good one."

"Huh? Oh.... sense, smell, I get it," not realizing that I had made a pun.

"My people did the same thing a long time ago when they were hunters on this land. Before a bear or deer hunt, they would cover themselves with mud. That would help hide their scent so they could stalk game more effectively."

"Maybe that's my problem. If I smear some fish smell all over myself, maybe I will catch something. Your folks lived around here?"

"My people lived all over Alabama, Georgia, Mississippi...."

"Dang! That's one big family," I said, confused.

"Yes it was. It was the entire Cherokee nation."

"Cherokee! You're an Indian?" I asked in disbelief.

"Well yes. Mostly Cherokee. My grandmother on my mother's side was Choctaw. So that makes me part Choctaw, but 100% Indian."

"Holy cow! I never met an Indian before. You don't look like an Indian."

"What do you think Indians should look like?"

"You know, moccasins, buckskin, eagle feathers, all that stuff."

"Son, you've been watching too many Roy Rogers movies. By the way, my name is Jack, Jack Feather," he said, extending his hand. "What's yours?"

"I'm Richard Dodge," I said as we shook hands. "But everyone calls me Rick. Nice to meet you, Mr. Feather."

I noticed Jack's hands were calloused and scarred, his fingers thick as sausages. These were hands that had seen many years of hard-scrabble living.

"Nice to meet you, Rick. However, please, call me Jack."

Jack sat down on the other end of my fishing log. While I fished, his dogs generally created havoc along the banks of the Warrior, and he proceeded to tell me his life story. Maybe it was because some people find it easier to talk to strangers, or perhaps he was just lonely, but he talked for over an hour. At first, I was put off by this interruption to my fishing, but then I began to listen. Jack was an only child. His mother had passed away from tuberculosis at a very young age, leaving him to fend for himself against an abusive, alcoholic father, and in a country that had no place for Indians.

"When Mom died, I actually lost both my parents. Dad was never the same after that," said Jack. "His only joy seemed to be drinking and beating me."

Jack's life suddenly changed one spring day when his father walked him to his grandmother's house, pressed a silver dollar into the palm of his hand, and disappeared. Four days later, his body was found floating in a west Alabama swamp. The official report was accidental drowning, but many believed it to be suicide.

"I know this is a horrible thing to say, but the only thing Dad ever gave me was a beating and that silver dollar the day he left. I've still got that dollar."

"Wow... that's... too bad." I always said the wrong things in these situations, and that sounded really stupid.

"Hey, I'm sorry to burden you with that. I don't know what came over me. I guess I haven't had any real company for a while. How old are you, Rick?"

"I'm thirteen and a half."

"You know, when I was your age, just about the turn of the century, things were very different. There was plenty of game, the rivers were full of fish, and there were still a few of my people living in these parts. I lived with my grandmother in her house, only a few miles from here. I remember, on more than one occasion, hearing mountain lions howling in the woods right around here. But those days are long gone," sighed Jack wistfully.

"I'm glad there aren't any mountain lions left."

"Why do you say that?" asked Jack.

"They scare the heck out of me."

"You're afraid of them only because you don't understand them. My grandfather believed that the spirits of Cherokee braves that died in battle returned as mountain lions."

"Do you believe that Jack?"

"Well, let's just say that there are a lot of things about this world that we do not understand. The Cherokee considered man, the earth, and the creatures as all simply different manifestations of the same thing. Everything was interconnected and interdependent; one animal was intimately intertwined with numerous others. Given that view of existence, it is not so far-fetched to suppose that life could flow from one form to another."

I had no idea what Jack was talking about, and he sensed my confusion.

"Let me ask you a question," said Jack. "Do you believe there is a heaven, a place where all the good people go after they die? Do you believe Moses parted the Red Sea and Jesus was the son of God and rose from the dead?"

"Of course I do, everyone knows those things."

"Then why can't my people believe that Cherokees return as creatures of the forest?"

"I reckon a man can believe whatever he wants in this country. But I wouldn't go spreading those things around. Folks will think you're nuts."

"People already think I'm nuts just because I'm an Indian."

"You don't seem crazy to me. Just a little confused."

Jack laughed out loud. "Well, thank you, Rick. But unfortunately, some folks are not as open-minded as you. Hey, you're about to catch a fish," said Jack suddenly.

I was staring directly at my fishing bobber when Jack made this proclamation, and I knew it had not moved at all. I was beginning to think Jack was more than a little confused.

"Jack, the float never moved, and I haven't had a bite…"

"Hush," said Jack. He was staring intently at the float, and I was feeling a little uneasy about Jack.

"Pull," said Jack. "Pull!"

"What? There's nothing there."

Jack reached over, and while I still held the pole, he gave it a quick jerk. The placid water suddenly came to life, and there, to my astonishment, was a good-sized fish hanging from my line.

"How in the world did you do that?"

"Oh, just lucky," said Jack smiling.

This would not be the last time that Jack would surprise me with his uncanny connection with the natural world. Jack was in tune with the rhythms of nature. He could predict the seasonal arrivals of migrating birds with amazing accuracy; he knew the best spots to find game, which plants could be used for treating various ailments, and he swore that he could smell a snake at 50 paces. He was the most consistent fisherman I ever met. Jack was as learned in the ways of nature as any formally educated professional.

In the beginning, I assumed that Jack's knowledge came from his many years spent observing and living close to nature. But later, I began to believe that there was something more to Jack's understanding of the ways of nature, a connection that I would never be able to share. I still wonder if Jack's almost supernatural abilities came, at least in part, because of his being descended from a people who relied upon the ability to recognize patterns in nature. To the Cherokee, knowing the ways of animals and the forces of wind and water was a matter of life and death.

"Oh crap, it's just a stupid drum," I said in disappointment. I tossed the fish onto the dusty riverbank and prepared to dispatch it with the heel of my shoe."

"Hold on," said Jack. "What are you doing?"

"I'm gonna smash its brains out. I wouldn't hit a hog in the butt with one of these. They're just trash fish."

"Don't kill it. Just toss it back."

"Hey, maybe it's one of your relatives come back as a fish?" I said teasingly.

Jack grinned. "You know, it does look a little like my Aunt Clara, rest her soul." Jack held the fish and looked it straight in the eye. "But Rick, why do you say they are no good? Sure, they are not all that good to eat, but like all things on this earth, they were put here for a purpose. It may not be obvious at times, but all animals have their place and their job to do. That fish is a bottom feeder and is sort of the 'garbage man' of the river, cleaning up all the trash left by other fish. What if all the drum were gone? We could be up to our necks in dead fish. The rivers would be a far less appealing place."

"Well, heck then, if you put it that way, I'll throw it back." I unceremoniously tossed the fish back into the Warrior, feeling a little embarrassed.

"Guess I better collect these crazy dogs and get on back. It has been a pleasure to meet you, Rick."

"Same here."

"If you are ever up around Lock 17, come on by the house and visit. I'll show you my moccasins and eagle feather headdress, and of course, I have lots of scalps hanging around," said Jack with a wink. "Ask anybody around, they can tell you where my house is."

"I might do that sometime," I said, as Jack walked toward his car.

Jack loaded his dogs into his old Dodge and drove away.

As I walked home that day, I couldn't stop thinking about Jack's tragic life, his strange appearance, and his mysterious beliefs. Up until that time, my life experiences were limited to uneventful small-town Alabama and the occasional motion picture. My comfortable life contrasted sharply with the hardships Jack had endured. The most perplexing thing, though, was the stunt he pulled with that fish. Maybe I just didn't see the float move, I thought. But that couldn't be. I was looking right at it. He probably saw the fish in the water, but the Warrior was so muddy you couldn't see anything. I couldn't come up with a reasonable explanation and decided to tell Dad about the entire event when I got home.

Chapter 2.

My Dad was a quiet man. When it came to the spoken word, he believed in quality over quantity, and when he spoke, everyone listened because most times he would say it only once. I have to admit that I did not always take the advice he handed out, and I often suffered for not taking it.

Dad lived his life on two basic principles. The first was that he treated everyone fairly and equally. With five children, it was important to him not to show favoritism. We all received equal shares of everything. The other principle was that he was true to his word. If Dad promised something, he would surely do it. This was a double-edged sword because when he said he would punish us for misbehavior, we knew it to be true.

After dinner that night, while Dad relaxed on the front porch, I brought up the encounter I had with Jack.

"I met an Indian down on the Warrior today while fishing."

"Jack Feather?" asked Dad.

"Yes, sir," I said, somewhat surprised. "How did you know?"

"I know he lives around there somewhere. Down at the plant, they say he's crazy and a roaring alcoholic to boot. Was he sober?"

"He seemed pretty normal, a regular guy, except he looks kind of weird. But that don't bother me none. He was very friendly. We talked about fishing mostly."

I thought it best not to tell Dad about the mountain lion thing.

"Dad, did you know that he was Cherokee, mostly, and that he has been living alone up near Lock 17 most all of his life? It must get mighty lonely up there all by yourself."

"Well. I probably shouldn't have said anything about that drinking thing. I shouldn't repeat what those guys say. Most of those fellas at work ain't got sense enough to pour pee out of a boot. For all I know, he has never drunk a drop in his life."

"Dad, Mr. Feather knows a lot about fishing and the river and stuff. He's lived there all his life. I never met an Indian before. He didn't look much like an Indian, though. He did the darndest thing. He knew I was about to get a bite before my bobber ever moved."

"Did I ever tell you that your great, great-grandmother on my side of the family was Cherokee?" asked Dad.

"No, I did not know that. Whoa, that's cool!"

"I never knew her because she passed away long before I was born, but I heard your grandfather talk about her. I don't know much about her, but I know she was a weaver. You know that blanket that Momma keeps in the cedar chest? She made that. That thing is over 100 years old, and it still looks like new. They also said that she preferred to eat a white dog over any other color of dog."

"That's disgusting. That's not really true, is it?"

"Well, that's what they say. That's probably just another one of those crazy things they say about folks when they don't fit their idea of how folks are supposed to look or act. There aren't many Indians left in these parts now, though," said Dad.

"What happened to them all?"

He paused to light another cigarette, leaned back in the porch chair, took a long, slow draw, and blew the smoke skyward. The cloud hung momentarily under the porch roof before slowly disappearing on the night breeze. I imagined I saw the ghostly shapes of Cherokee braves in the dissipating smoke.

"Well, it's a pretty sorry thing, what we did to the Indians son. The government rounded up as many as they could and forced them out of this part of the country. Made them walk all the way to Oklahoma, in the dead of winter, and put them on reservations. Women, children, everybody. Lots of them died before they ever got there. They called it the Trail of Tears. I am surprised that some of Jack's relatives managed to escape the removal."

"I heard about that in school. Do you think some of Jack's relatives died?"

"I wouldn't be surprised," said Dad. "The government treated the Indians like dirt. It has always been a mystery to me how the same politicians who was trying to free the slaves, were, at the same time, trying to wipe out the Indians. It just don't make no sense to me."

I was glad that Dad was not overly concerned with my meeting with Jack because I had every intention of learning more about Jack and the Cherokee.

C hapter 3.

The very next weekend, I found my way up to Lock 17 to look up Jack. After searching for some time, I finally found the house that I believed was his. It was at the end of a long dirt road that ran along a small creek. Large Cypress trees lined the banks. It was small, and its grey, weathered exterior suggested that it had never had a coat of paint. There was a small truck patch at one side of the house. Several sets of deer antlers, bleached white from the sun, were nailed to the exterior. The house was set upon stacks of fieldstones gathered from the surrounding woods. When Jack's dogs came barking from under the house, I knew I had the right place. Jack peered suspiciously from the open door, his expression changing when he recognized me.

"Hi, Mr. Feather, I hope you don't mind me dropping by. You said to look you up if I was up this way."

"Well, hello, Rick", replied Jack. "I thought you might be one of those fellows from down at the fishing camp. I don't get a lot of social calls out here. Come up on the porch and take a load off. Are you hungry?"

"No, sir. I just had lunch a little bit ago. But thanks for the offer."

"How did you do fishing the other day? Did you catch anything else after I left?"

"Nah," I said disgustedly. "Most times when I go fishing, I can't even catch a cold."

"Hey, I've got an idea. You want to go catch some fish right now?" asked Jack. "I think the conditions are just about right for us to have some good luck."

"If you're waiting on me, you're backing up," I said excitedly.

Jack and I walked down a small path that led from his house to the riverbank, and there, tied to a cypress tree, was an old wooden boat. Two oars lay across the seat. Partially filled with water, it looked like it might sink at any minute. It was obviously hand-made, and I had never seen a worse excuse for a vessel, at least not one that was actually floating.

"Dang, is that your boat?" I asked in disbelief. "We're going out in the river in that!"

"That's it. I call her Marie, after my Granny. I've been a thousand miles in that boat and caught ten times that many fish in it."

"*Titanic* would be a better name," I retorted.

"You don't have to worry. She's very seaworthy, just a little leaky, like Granny was," joked Jack.

I started giggling, which started Jack laughing, and soon we were both belly laughing to beat the band.

We climbed into the boat and sat down, Jack in the rear and I on the middle seat. Jack handed me an old rusty coffee can.

"Your job at the moment is to bail this water out while I row us up-river a little. You'll have to keep your eye on the water level and bail it out every so often. Don't drop that can overboard either, or our fishing trip will be over."

I untied Marie, Jack pulled a few times on the oars, and we were out in the main current of the Warrior. As we pulled away from the shore, it occurred to me that the only thing in the boat, besides a lot of holes, was a piece of rope, a rusty can, and two oars.

"Jack, how in the world are we gonna fish? Unless you got some dynamite in your back pocket, we ain't got a single piece of fishing gear."

"You've probably never caught fish the way we are gonna do it today," said Jack.

"Is this gonna be some kind of Indian thing?" I asked.

"You might say that," replied Jack. "You don't mind getting wet, do you?"

"Heck no, not me! My Mom says I was practically borned with webbed feet and gills."

"That's good because what we are gonna do is be really quiet, and pull up to that submerged weed bed over there," explained Jack as he pointed toward a patch of weeds, their emerald green tops emerging from the brown water. "When we get there, I will climb out of the boat and stand close to the weed bed. I'm gonna say some magical Indian words, and that will cause any fish that are there to jump into the boat. You need to hold onto that overhanging tree limb to keep the boat from drifting while the fish jump in. When they do, just grab them before they flop out. Do you think you can handle that?" asked Jack.

"Okay, let me get this straight. The fish are gonna just jump into the boat?" I asked in disbelief. "Is that what you are saying to me?"

"That is exactly what I am saying, Rick," whispered Jack as he eased himself over the side of the boat into the water.

"Will these fish be alive?" I whispered. "Or will they be served up fried with hush puppies and cheese grits?"

Jack, about chest deep in water, gave me a wink and began a repetitious chant.

"Da-li, a-mo, da-li, wa-ti, da-li, a-mo, da-li, wa-ti."

Dang, I was feeling very self-conscious and looked up and down the river, hoping no one would come along and see me here. I was beginning to wonder if Jack might have a few loose bolts.

Jack continued for a few moments, and suddenly a small bass leapt from the water, hit the side of the boat with a thud, and fell back into the river.

"That one was too small anyway," pronounced Jack. "I'll try again."

Okay, that was weird, I thought. *Probably just a coincidence. There is no way that he is gonna get fish to jump into this boat.*

Jack pushed the boat ahead about one boat length and began his chanting again. Suddenly, a large carp leapt straight out of the water, rising to just about head height. Jack, in one swift motion, caught the fish in mid-air and pushed it over into the boat. It lay at my feet, crimson gills flashing and tail slapping at the water that was pooled there. I was getting a soaking. I immediately pounced on the fish to subdue it.

Jack began laughing as he watched my attempts at restraining the large, slimy fish.

"Don't let him get the best of you, Rick. You can take him," said Jack in mock encouragement.

I finally managed to get the fish in my spindly arms when Jack said, "If you are finished playing with it, you can throw it back."

"You let me get soaking wet, and all slimed up," I said exhausted, "and now we are gonna just throw it back?"

"Carp are really tasty fish, but they are so bony that I hate to mess with them. Just toss it back in, and we will get something better."

"Holy cow! How in the world did you do that?"

"I didn't do it," said Jack. "The fish did. I just gave it a little Indian encouragement. Those Cherokee words you hear me saying, I am actually speaking to the fish. I tell him that the Great Spirit of the River has turned the river upside down, and the water is now the air and the air is now the water, and if he does not hurry and leap into the water, he will surely die. The fish get very excited and confused when I tell them that, and they jump straight up and into our boat."

"You can actually talk to fish!" I asked in disbelief.

"Can't you?" replied Jack. A smile cracked across his face and then grew into full laughter.

"Alright, tell me what is going on here," I asked indignantly.

It took a bit for Jack to catch his breath, but then he explained.

"Well, spooking fish is pretty simple. If you had paid closer attention, you would have seen that I was holding one of the boat paddles under the water. When I started singing that Cherokee song, I ran the paddle into that weed bed as if I was thrusting a sword. The fish feel the water move or the paddle actually touches them, and they take off like a rocket. Often as not, they go straight up, and sometimes, they land in our boat. It ain't very sportsmen-like, but it can be a lot of fun, and it's a good way to get dinner."

"Can I try it?"

"Sure you can," said Jack. "Let's pull up to that next weed bed and give it a go."

After several failed attempts, a decent-sized bass fell into the boat. At the end of the day, we had two bass, and I had an adventure I would not soon forget. We returned to Jack's house, where he cleaned the fish and prepared them with fried potatoes and coffee.

After supper, Jack and I sat on the porch of his old house for most of that afternoon and talked about the Cherokee, fishing, and most everything else. He showed me a few fading photos of his relatives. In every face, I could see the same physical features that I saw in Jack. When I told Jack that I was distantly related to the Cherokee, he was truly excited, insisting that he had sensed my Indian blood all along.

"Rick, I think we should give you a name befitting your newly discovered heritage. An Indian name. What do you think?" said Jack.

"Wow! That would be so cool. What do you think would be a good name? Man, this is so neat." I could hardly contain myself.

"Cherokee names were given to describe the physical features of the bearer or perhaps to honor some exceptional physical prowess. What about Ta-ja-na-ga-la?"

"Ta-ja-na-ga-la. That sounds really neat."

I kept repeating the name using the deepest baritone my adolescent vocal cords could muster.

"What does it mean?"

"Ta-ja-na-ga-la means *Man with Fish Lips*."

"Huh"? I don't think I like that one too much," I said, feeling rather deflated.

Jack was grinning from ear to ear and watching my reaction. I then realized he was kidding.

"Ha ha, very funny," I said sarcastically.

"O.K., how about A-mo-ga-yu-hi? That means 'Running Water'. I think that fits you. We first met on the banks of the river, and when you are on that bike of yours, you are fast like running water. What do you think?"

"I love it."

"Alright, then Running Water it is," proclaimed Jack.

"But shouldn't we have some kind of a ceremony? Kill a buffalo? Pluck feathers out of an eagle's butt? Something?"

"Well, since both Eagles and Buffalo are protected by law, it might not be a good idea to mess around with them. Tell you what, you come back just before sunset next Saturday, and I will tell you all I know about Cherokee ceremonies. I think you might find it interesting."

"Cool!" Do you mind if I bring my cousin Donnie Green? He loves Indian stuff?"

"No problem," said Jack. "Is he related to Minzo Green?"

"Yes, sir, that's his dad."

"Minzo's a good man."

"I think everybody likes Mr. Green. Did you know that he was the coroner?"

"Yes, I did. I voted for him in the last election. Tell him I said hello the next time you see him."

"I'll do that. I guess I better head to the house. Thanks for the supper. I'll see you later."

"See you. Be careful on that bicycle!"

"I will." I jumped on my bike and headed down the dusty river road, Jack's dogs running alongside.

C hapter 4.
Among my circle of friends, Donnie was the fellow that I was always getting into trouble with. When we were together, it was like mixing matter and anti-matter. You just shouldn't put the two of them together, and if you did, the outcome was not going to be good. Don't get me wrong, we never did anything intentionally bad; it seemed that we were just always making bad judgments. It seemed that trouble followed us everywhere.

Donnie stood in the front yard and shouted at the open screen door of my house. "Elmword! Mom says you can come over and have dinner with us."

Donnie wore cut-offs, a t-shirt, and dirty tennis shoes. His curly brown hair, cropped short on the sides and long on top, made his head seem unusually elongate. Donnie sometimes called me "Elmwood", after a local cemetery, because he was convinced that my behavior would lead me to an early grave. However, Donnie had the peculiar habit of inserting an "r" into certain words such that the name came out as "Elmword". One of Donnie's favorite words was "beautiful," but it came out as "brootiful".

Despite Donnie's speech impediment, he was an amazing harmonica player. Not only was he an exceptional player, but he also played the instrument in a manner that no one had ever played before. The harmonica was very small, and he would put the entire thing in his mouth and, manipulating it with his tongue, would play it with no hands. This freed up his hands to engage in other activities. He could play *Turkey in the Straw* while taking a bath or *Silent Night* while picking blackberries. I recall one particular occasion while playing baseball. The pitcher for our team, the Hueytown Golden Gophers, had a no-hitter late in the bottom of the ninth inning. Donnie was playing center field when the batter hit a high pop fly. Donnie took out across the field playing "The Star

Spangled Banner" as he ran. He made a diving catch and landed face down in a turnip patch. He didn't miss the catch, and he didn't miss a note.

"Dad, can I spend the night at Donnie's?" I asked.

"I don't mind, replied Dad, but I don't want a repeat of last time."

The words were barely out of his mouth when I banged through the front screen door. I knew that when Donnie asked if I wanted to come over, it was actually code for *let's find trouble to get into*. Dad's warning referred to the fact that we had started a small forest fire when Donnie and I were last together. While playing a game that we called *Smoke Jumpers*, we managed to set the woods on fire. The rules of the game were simple. One person, with a pack of matches, would run through the forest starting small fires while the other would follow, close on his heels, beating them out with a pine branch. We only played this game once because we soon realized that it had a fundamental flaw: the person with the matches could start fires much faster than the fellow with the pine branch could put them out. The first few fires were easy to contain, but, despite my best efforts with the pine branch, the fires grew larger and larger until a neighbor, who saw the smoke rising, called the volunteer fire department. The fire was under control in no time and was nothing compared to the fire my dad lit across my backside when I got home.

In the waning evening light, Donnie and I trotted across the field that separated our houses.

"You gotter see the neat stuff Dad has in the utilerty room", said Donnie excitedly. "He goes in there and stays for hours. I just gotter know what it is he does in there. I think it's Private Dertective stuff."

Donnie told everyone his dad was a "Private Detective" because we frankly had no idea what a Coroner actually did. We knew it had something to do with police work, but that was about it.

"Let's sneak in and check it out after dinner," I suggested.

"He locks it every night."

"I'll find a way to get in," I said confidently.

"Brootiful!" said Donnie.

After a dinner of ham, biscuits, and tomato gravy, I despised tomato gravy, we rushed outside." We sat in the grass and watched fireflies drift across the cow pasture that bordered Donnie's backyard. I told him all about my encounter with Jack Feather.

"Jack gave me an Indian name, and this Saturday night he is gonna do some Indian stuff at his house down on the Warrior River. I asked him if you could come along and he said that would be great. He actually knows your Dad," I explained.

"Cool!" said Donnie. "Do you think he will give me an Indian name, too? Maybe something like Frying Eagle or Rone Worf."

"You mean Lone Wolf."

"That's what I said, Lone Worf."

"Whatever. I am sure he'll give you a cool name. He's a really nice guy. He knows all about fishing and nature and stuff."

"I don't know if dad will let me," said Donnie.

"Tell your dad that you'll be at my house and I'll tell my Dad that I'll be at yours."

"Sounds good to me. I'll ask him tonight. Now let's see if we can get into that utilerty room."

A small window in the utility room was open and just large enough to admit a couple of 13-year-olds. Donnie, being a bit taller, boosted me through the window and climbed in after. We dropped to the floor of the darkened room. Donnie found the light and switched it on. The blood red light of the photographic dark room revealed pictures that were hung around the room on clotheslines to dry. We both gasped as the images of the photos leapt out at us from every direction. A body missing most of the left side of its head, a swollen, decomposing drowning victim, a car crash victim whose body, so entwined within twisted metal, made it virtually impossible to tell where the human being stopped and the automobile began. The room began to feel uncomfortably hot and clammy.

"GOOD GRIEF!" cried Donnie in disgust. "What in the world does Dad have all these gross pictures for?"

"Beats me," I said, shaking my head. "I guess it has something to do with his job. Detectives have to investigate murders and stuff to try to find out how somebody died. These are probably just pictures he had to take at work."

"Donnie, look here, if you cover this big hole up in the head of this guy with your finger, it looks like Coach Blockner. Wasn't he absent from gym class last Friday?"

"That doesn't look like Croach," said Donnie. "Croach has blonde hair, this poor sap has red hair."

"Donnie, everything in the room is red."

"Good point," admitted Donnie.

Most of the equipment was large and ominous-looking. The closest thing we had ever seen to this was Dr. Frankenstein's lab in the movies. Strange chemicals lined the shelves. One large, brightly colored can caught my eye.

"Hey, look at this, Z-O-L-O-X," I spelled slowly. "What does that mean?"

"Durned if I know," said Donnie, who was absorbed by his examination of a photographic enlarger.I removed the cap with some difficulty and sniffed the contents. "Gag a maggot, it smells like your mom's tomato gravy."

"Quiet," whispered Donnie, "somebody's coming."

We heard the back door slam and someone calling Donnie's name.

"Oh great," It's Bung-Hole," said Donnie. "What the heck does he want?"

"Bung-Hole" was the nickname that Donnie used for his little brother, Ronnie. Ronnie was only two years younger, but we treated him like he was contagious. Bung-hole was actually short for Bung-holeum, and Bung-holeum was short for Bung-holeum, linoleum, petroleum, mongoleum. We teased Ronnie with that name because it made him really angry.

For some reason, Donnie grabbed the can of ZOLOX, and we scampered out the window into the back yard just as Ronnie rounded the corner.

"Hey, what-cha got there?" asked Ronnie.

"It's ZOLOX," I said.

"What's it for?" asked Ronnie, one finger jammed up his nose.

"You don't know squat, Bung-hole," insisted Donnie. "ZOLOX is Dertective stuff."

"Yea, it's Detective stuff," I parroted haughtily.

"It looks like the stuff that Dad uses to light the barbecue grill. Let's see if it will burn," suggested Ronnie.

We were always burning stuff. Hula Hoops were the best. Once you get one lit, the melted plastic would drip to the ground and make the strangest sound, as well as an amazing nighttime light show. We called a piece of burning Hula Hoop a "Zorch" because the dripping, burning, molten plastic made a strange sound as it fell to the ground, sort of like that word. However, we found out the hard way that if any of the burning plastic got on your skin, it was the worst pain you would ever experience. You had to be very careful with a Zorch."

We squirted some ZOLOX on the grass and threw a match on it. The ZOLOX burned, producing various shades of blue, yellow, green, and red. In the darkness of Donnie's backyard, the effect was spectacular. Like a fireworks show in microcosm.

"Whoa, that's brootiful!" said Donnie.

Many paradoxes in the world have taxed the minds of great scientists; the origin of the universe and the meaning of life, to name a couple. Ranking right up there with these complex questions is the workings of the juvenile brain. What inspired Donnie to squirt ZOLOX on his P.F. Flyer tennis shoes and set them on fire, I'll never know. He buck-danced around the back yard, screaming in mock pain.

"Yaaaaaaaaaaaaaaaaarrrr!" yelled Donnie as he ran around like his mind was rented out.

"Man, are you crazy?" I asked in disbelief.

Donnie, paying no attention to me, continued to buck-dance and scream. The flame on his shoes burned quickly and immediately went out. We discovered that one of the properties of ZOLOX was that, perhaps due to its extreme volatility, it apparently did not produce a great deal of heat when applied sparingly. After Donnie's feat of flaming feet, we became bolder. We took turns dousing our tennis shoes, setting them on fire, and dashing around the darkened back yard. The trick was not to use too much ZOLOX and to move your feet fast enough that the flames were quickly extinguished. We locked arms and did a flaming do-si-do square dance.

"Swing your partner round-and-round," sang Donnie.

"Hey, let me do it," insisted Ronnie.

Donnie doused Bung-holes' tennis shoes, turned to look at me, and said, "Please do not try this at home; we are trained professionals."

In his exuberance, Donnie drenched Ronnie's left pants leg, and I lit him aflame. We watched Bung-hole race around the back yard like a low-flying comet as the flames rose up his pant leg. This was the best one of all we thought. Donnie, visibly moved by the spectacle, said, "Wow, that's brootiful. He looks like the Human Torch."

Ronnie began running faster and faster, but the flames would not go out. He began to frantically beat on his flaming leg and foot with no results. Ronnie would stop, bend over, beat on his leg, and run like crazy, stop, beat, run like crazy. Donnie and I fell to the ground laughing, the kind of laughter that is so intense that no sound comes out of your mouth. We thought this was the funniest thing we had ever seen. Donnie, between belly laughs, breathlessly shouted encouragement:

"Run, Bung-hole!" Run!"

Perhaps due to the pants leg beating or the incredible speed at which Ronnie was racing around the yard, the possibility entered our juvenile brains that he was not enjoying this as much as we were.

"Donnie," I said, "I think he is really on fire".

"Nah, he ain't," said Donnie, "you know how Bung-hole lies".

After conferring on the matter for a few moments more, we decided that rather than run the risk of burning up Donnie's only brother and, perhaps more importantly, run the risk of getting our butts beaten once again, we would assist in extinguishing him. The problem was the speed at which he was coursing around the back yard.

It is amazing how fast even the most unathletic individual can run when he or she is on fire. I suggest that strategically applied ZOLOX could guarantee that American athletes would bring home significantly more medals in Olympic events. Particularly those that involved running and jumping. The opening ceremonies and the lighting of the Olympic flame would certainly take on new significance.

We waited until Ronnie's orbit around the back yard passed close to us, and we began the chase. After pursuing him for what seemed like forever, Donnie finally tackled him, and we rolled him around in the damp grass of an Alabama summer night.

Amidst the sound of whimpering, flailing of limbs, and the smell of burnt hair, we examined him for damage. There on his calf was a large red blister.

"Whoa! Man!" Look at that blister," I said. "It looks just like South America."

Donnie and I thought that blister was pretty neat. Ronnie, however, could not appreciate the moment as much as we. He headed, whimpering, for the back door and, upon entering the house, screamed;

"MOMMA! DONNIE TRIED TO BURN ME UP!"

"DONNIE!", bellowed Mrs. Green, "GET YOUR REAR IN THIS HOUSE RIGHT NOW!"

That was my cue to head for home.

Chapter 5

Jack fed another log on the fire, sending a swarm of sparks rocketing into the clear night sky. Flames greedily attacked the dry pine, forcing the encroaching darkness back beyond the stark pines and oaks standing sentinel at the edge of Jack's backyard. Frog song and a thin, damp fog drifted up from the banks of the Warrior River. A sliver of a moon hung high in the cloudless sky, marred only by the column of smoke rising from our campfire.

Our ruse had worked, and Donnie and I had stolen away to meet Jack. We sat around a fire that Jack had going before we arrived. The campfire bathed Jack in an ethereal orange light and accentuated his otherworldly appearance as he began to speak.

"Unfortunately, many of the customs and beliefs of the Cherokee have been lost for all times," said Jack.

"Why is that, Jack?" asked Donnie.

"Well, the Cherokee did not write things down as we do now. Much of their history was passed down in songs and stories told by one generation to the next. Over the years, people have died and taken most of Cherokee history to their graves."

"Don't you know any of the stories?" I asked.

"I know a few, but I never knew most of them because my grandmother didn't tell me. She probably did not know all of them either," added Jack

"But I do know some interesting things about the Cherokee. For instance, water was sacred to the Cherokee. That's probably why I have always lived near water, and I love going out on the river in *Marie*," said Jack as he pushed a stick into the fire with his foot.

"Yeah, Donnie," I said, "You should see *Marie*, Jack's boat. It's a real yacht."

"The Cherokee had a saying that, when translated into English, basically meant, *Go to water*," continued Jack. "What that means is that no matter what your problem is, the river or the ocean, or even a creek would help you solve it. I want you boys to always remember that. The river has always helped me, and I hope you will always respect it."

"Hey, I grot no probrem with going to water," said Donnie. "If something is bothering you, just go frishing. If you ask me, the Cherokee was very smart forks," quipped Donnie.

"You mean smart folks," corrected Jack.

"That's what I said, smart forks," said Donnie.

Jack gave me an odd look, and I giggled a little.

"Even today, many Cherokee believe that moving water is sacred and going to water is a very respected tradition," added Jack. "When someone dies, the family members of the deceased are expected to immerse themselves seven times in the river. When they came out, it was like being cleansed."

"Hey, that's sort of like gettin' Babertized," said Donnie. "The Preacher sometimes Babertizes forks in an old strip mine near our church."

Jack turned and gave me a confused look.

"He means Baptized folks," I whispered.

"Oh," said Jack, nodding his head.

"The Cherokee also believed that good people, who lived their lives right, went to a place that was always filled with light and was pleasant, and bad people would go to a place of pain, and they would be tortured. Does that sound familiar?" asked Jack.

"Sounds like Heaven and H-e-double-toothpicks to me," I said.

"Exactly", said Jack. "And you know the Cherokee also believed that the spirit of a man could take different forms. My grandmother told me that some believed that brave Cherokee warriors would return to earth in the form of a mountain lion. Both the owl and the mountain lion were sacred animals to the Cherokee."

Donnie and I looked around nervously and then moved closer to Jack.

"Another Cherokee belief was that some plants were sacred. For example, have you boys ever seen cedar wood?" asked Jack.

"Sure," said Donnie. "My Moms got a cedar chest, but it makes our blankets smell kind of funky."

"The Cherokee thought that the cedar tree was the most sacred of all plants because of its wood. Cedar wood is red and white, and those two colors were important for the Cherokee. As a matter of fact, cedar wood was used to carry the dead to honor them. Also, fire was very important to the Cherokee. They believed that it was a gift from God directly to the Cherokee," said Jack.

"You know, I've always been crazy about fire," I said, staring into the hypnotic flames. "Me and Donnie used to burn up all kinds of stuff."

"Well, you boys know you have to be careful with fire. Don't let me catch you doing anything foolish. You have to respect fire the same way you respect water," said Jack as he secretly slipped his hand into his pants pocket.

"Fire is one of the things that separates us from the animals, but it has to be respected. If you take it for granted, you can get hurt real bad."

With those words, Jack tossed a handful of grey powder that he had extracted from his pants pocket into the fire.

WHOOSH!!!!!!!!

The blinding flash threw Donnie and me on our backsides. Jack fell backwards off his log and began laughing. A mushroom cloud of sulfur smoke rose from the campfire.

"What the heck was that?" I asked as I picked myself up from the ground.

Donnie said nothing; his eyes, as big as dinner plates, spoke volumes.

"That was an old Medicine Man trick," said Jack as he brushed himself off. "I threw some gunpowder into the fire to liven things up. Sort of gets your attention, don't it?"

"You could say that," said Donnie, regaining his composure.

"I didn't mean to use that much. It scared the heck out of me, too," added Jack.

After that, we both begged Jack to give us some gunpowder so we could throw it in the fire, but he refused.

"I almost blew us all up, and you boys want to do it again? And they say that Indians are crazy," said Jack. "Black powder is dangerous, so you can just get that thought out of your heads."

"Could I ask you boys a favor?" said Jack.

"Sure thing. What is it?" said Donnie

"I don't have any relatives, and you boys are the only friends I have. Now I ain't saying I am gonna be kicking the bucket any time soon, but I worry about not having a proper Cherokee burial, like my grandmother told me about. I know this is a big favor to ask, but when I pass away, could you boys see that I get planted right over there behind my house? I've already dug the grave, and when they bury me, just tell them to place my head so that it is facing west, shovel some dirt in on top of me, and then take all those rocks in that pile there and mound them on top. I hold the deed to this house and land, and although the state of Alabama will probably take it when I die, at least the part that I am buried on can't be touched. Alabama law says that a grave is protected ground and can't be disturbed. And you know, since Minzo is the County Coroner, he probably knows how to get this done. Donnie, would you ask him about this?"

"I can ask him", said Donnie. "But dorn't you warnna be buried in that brig church graveyard over across town?"

"No, I don't, Donnie. I want to know that this tiny piece of Alabama will always be Cherokee land. They can't take that away, no matter what," added Jack, his face darkening as the fire died somewhat. "Would you boys promise to do that for me? It's really important to me."

That night, two young boys made a promise to ease an old man's mind. A promise that they hoped they would never have to keep.

C hapter 6
Without question, some of the most pleasurable times of my life have been those spent while on, around, or in the water. In fact, an early fascination with the creatures that inhabited the fresh waters of rural Alabama inextricably drew me to any and every body of water that was within range of my bicycle.

Although my friends and I gigged bull frogs, captured tadpoles, and chased turtles up and down countless muddy river banks, I was especially fond of fish and fishing. I knew the lakes that were the haunts of largemouth bass and bream, the creeks where minnows and chubs swam in thick, shimmering schools, and the rivers that were the havens for catfish large enough to swallow a man's leg.

It should come as no surprise that I would always jump at the opportunity to go fishing. Two of my favorite fishing partners were Donnie and his dad, Minzo. Minzo drove a 1955 Buick Roadmaster he called his fishing car; we kids called it the Dirt Dauber because it was always covered with red Alabama clay. When the dirt was removed, the car was a dark green that reminded me of the sluggish waters of the Warrior River, one of our favorite fishing destinations. The first time I sat in that car, I was surprised to discover that a car I thought was an antique had air conditioning, power seats, power brakes, power steering, and, most impressive of all, power windows. My Dad's 1965 Ford had none of these amenities.

So, on a steamy June morning, Uncle Minzo, Donnie, Jack, and I loaded the Dirt Dauber with fishing rods, tackle boxes, soft drinks, sandwiches, tins of sardines, and cans of potted meat and Vienna sausages. With all the gear in place, we motored out of residential Hueytown and within minutes hit the rolling countryside, the early morning sun rising in the rear window. Hank Williams crooned *Poor Ole Cauliga* over the AM radio as Minzo got the *Roadmaster* up to cruising speed. The old car strained to pull the hills of west Alabama and seemed to breathe a sigh of relief as it dropped into the cool, mist-filled valleys.

As we breezed along Birmingport Highway, I watched through the open window as the landscape alternated between fertile fields of corn and cotton, thick pine forests, great strip-mined gashes in the earth, surreal landscapes of smothering Kudzu, and the ramshackle houses of poor black farmers. As we approached the Warrior River, our progress slowed as the road became more treacherous and the smell of the river bottom enveloped us. Our pulses quickened, as, from atop the last hill that marked the eastern edge of the Warrior flood plain, across the tops of ancient fog-shrouded oaks and sycamores, we caught a brief glimpse of the river stretching out below us silvery in the early morning sun.

The last few miles to the river always seemed to take the longest, but with tires crunching on gravel, Minzo finally pulled the *Roadmaster* into the parking lot of *The Bullfrog Fishing Camp and Social Club*. The Bullfrog was a popular spot for local fishermen, and the Social Club, for those looking for game of another kind, namely, moonshine whiskey. Every Friday and Saturday night at the Social Club, many mason jars of corn liquor were served up to anyone with a few dollars. The remains of the previous night's celebration littered the riverbank. A disheveled patron staggered near the water's edge and, as we got out of the Dirt Dauber, began moving in our direction.

I was absolutely amazed by the spectacle. This fellow was as drunk as one could possibly be and still remain standing. His movements were "Gumby-like", as if there was not a bone in his entire body. He wore a dirty, green "John Deere" baseball cap, a soiled t-shirt, and brown polyester pants. His fly was down, and his boxer shorts were pulled partway out of the opening as if he had made an unsuccessful attempt at urinating. He wore no shoes and had but a single brown sock on his left foot. Strangest of all was the bedraggled bouquet of plastic flowers that he clutched to his chest. As he made his way toward us, this cartoon character of a man steadied himself on tree and fence post, and finally fell across the hood of the Dirt Dauber. It seemed that it required a Herculean effort to cover the 50 feet from the riverbank to the car.

"Good Lord! Is that you, D.W.?" said Minzo, who apparently knew every soul in Jefferson County, Alabama.

"You boys stay in the car while Jack and I speak with Mr. Garret. I don't think he is feeling very well." Donnie and I sat and snickered quietly.

D.W. Garret was the local insurance agent, a member of the First Baptist Church, and a volunteer of the Rock Creek Volunteer Fire Department. A veritable pillar of the community for six days of the week, come Friday night, D.W. warmed a bar stool at the Social Club.

"Look at those devilish ducks," slurred D.W. draped across the fender of the Buick and pointing at the Mergansers that waddled along the bank.

"D.W., you look like crap," said Minzo in disgust. "Does Betty know where you are?"

"You better... urp... watch those devilish ducks," hiccupped D.W., obviously paying no attention to Minzo whatsoever.

Minzo and Jack each took an arm and, with more than a little difficulty, began to escort D.W. to the Social Club.

"You boys go ahead and load the gear into that first boat over there while we take care of D.W. He's not feeling well," said Minzo. "If you want to sit in the boat, go ahead, but put those life jackets on. This won't take long".

As they slowly made their way inside, Donnie and I loaded one of the boats that Minzo rented from the fish camp. The boats were wooden, flat-bottomed, and painted dark green, their only means of propulsion being oars. I suspected that the main reason Minzo took us kids along on these trips was free labor, because we rowed him for many hours up and down the Warrior River. Anxious to begin fishing, we loaded in record time, donned our life jackets, and took our places in the boat. Half an hour later, with tackle laid out and fishing poles ready, there was no sign of Minzo.

"Where the heck are they?" I said to no one in particular. "Donnie, go into the Social Club and see what's keeping him."

"No way, man," said Donnie, "I'm not about to gro in there. They're probably sucking down whiskey with D.W. by now."

"Crap! crap! crap! We're burning up valuable fishing time. To heck with this," I said. "I'm gonna fish right here!"

"How you gronna do that?" asked Donnie. "Dad didn't buy no bait yet!"

"We got sardines, don't we!"

"Oh yeah sure, you'll catch plenty on that", said Donnie sarcastically.

"Hey, it's better than sitting here with our thumbs up our butts."

Taking Minzo's heaviest cane pole, I popped open a can, selected a plump sardine, and skewered it with a sizeable hook. Sitting in the bow of the boat and dropping the bait into the murky depths right at the end of the dock, I locked my gaze onto the red and white bobber, ready to detect the slightest vibration. Sometime later, with not even a nibble, I began nibbling the sardines myself.

"Elmword, I know your problem," said Donnie, "you forgot to put a cracker and some ketchup on that hook, hee, hee, hee," snickered Donnie.

"Real funny!" You're gonna crap when I catch something." I withdrew my fishing line from the water to find a completely bare hook.

"Well shoot! I'm fishing on credit."

Swinging the hook into the boat, I fitted it with another sardine, increased the depth of the hook by sliding the bobber up the line, and tossed it out again.

Donnie, now lying across the boat seat, took out his harmonica and began playing *Away in a Manger*, loudly. I ignored the racket until I couldn't take it anymore.

"Donnie! Shut the heck up!!" I demanded. "If there were any fish around here, they are long gone by now."

"O.K., O.K.!! Good grief, everybody's a darn critic," lamented Donnie. "Give me that lunch bag, I'm hungry." Donnie took the bag, extracted a can of Royal Crown Cola, a sandwich, and a large pepper, and began eating noisily.

"Whew-wee, this pepper is as hot as a two-dollar pistol." Donnie broke the pepper open, scraped the fiery seeds out, and ate only the "cooler" portion of the pepper.

"Man, that's a hot prepper," said Donnie as he chugged some Royal Crown.

Donnie hastily drank the remainder of the cola, trying to extinguish the burn. "I shouldn't have et that pepper. Man, I'm gonner regret it later."

"Donnie, would you try to hold the noise down to a roar? I'm trying to fish."

"Complain, complain," said Donnie as he stood on the boat's rear seat. "I gotter take a leak."

"Well, don't do it here!"

"Too late," answered Donnie as he let it fly over the side of the boat. "There's no stopping it now".

Donnie finished his business, zipped up, broke-wind, and sat down again.

"Where the heck is Minzo, doggone it!! I'm about fed up with this crap," complained Donnie. He was by now fidgeting nervously in the boat seat, causing the boat to rock slightly. I looked back to see him red-faced and sweating. With legs crossed, he squirmed around on the back seat of the boat.

"Elmword, I think something is wrong."

"Your darn right something is wrong!! We been sitting here forever and we ain't even left the dock."

"No, not that. I mean.....uh........ I got this funny feeling." Donnie jabbed his hands into the front of his pants.

Suddenly, my fishing bobber went under and immediately returned to the surface. I placed both hands on the cane pole and waited.

"Donnie, I just got a bite," I whispered, hoping not to scare away whatever had just sampled my sardine.

"It's probably just an old river turtle," said Donnie in an agitated voice.

The words were barely out of his mouth when the bobber shot out of sight. I pulled on the pole to "set the hook" and felt something pull back ferociously. The fishing pole bent double under the weight of something very large swam around the end of the dock, stretching my line across the pier pilings.

"Holy cow! Donnie, I got something! Untie the boat before it breaks my line on this pier".

Donnie absentmindedly followed orders and pulled the boat closer to the end of the dock. At this point, the fish must have sensed something because it struck out for open water and I hung on like stink on a pole cat. The fish, towing us along, pulled away from the dock and headed down the Warrior River.

Chapter 7

Minzo and Jack sat at the bar of the "Social Club" pouring black coffee into D.W., much of it cascading down the front of his dirty t-shirt. Still clutching the bouquet of plastic flowers, D.W. slumped face down across the bar. Travis McBride, the proprietor of the Bull Frog, looked on from behind the bar. Crew-cut hair, square jaw, arms like the limbs of an oak tree, Travis was an ex-golden gloves boxer and a mountain of a man. Unfortunately, over time, much of the flesh at higher altitudes had avalanched to rest in his large gut. Nevertheless, he was still an imposing individual, and few men were brave enough to square off with him.

The Social Club smelled of fish bait, cigarettes, and last night's corn whiskey. The latter, emanating mostly from D.W. A Wallace for President bumper sticker, was stuck on the back of the 1930s cash register. Numerous others adorned the walls of the establishment; I Brake for Fresh Road-Kill, and Keep America Beautiful, Shoot a Hippie, some of the more notable. A large window behind the bar looked out upon the Warrior River.

"Now darn it D.W., we got to get you sobered up, said Minzo as he raised D.W.'s head from the bar to slog more coffee in him. "Betty was worried sick when I called her and she asked me to take care of you and by George I aim to do it."

With a look of wild terror in his eyes D.W. suddenly grabbed Jack by the arm and in whisky garbled words said, "Them ducks, them ducks is after me, don't let 'em get me please, PLEASE!!!". He frantically waved the bouquet of flowers in the air as if defending against a swarm of bees.

"Don't worry D.W., we won't let them get you. Just calm down," said Jack.

D.W. grabbed Jack by his shirt and pulled him over to him so that they were nose-to-nose. D.W. stared Jack square in the eye and asked. "You an injun ain't you?"

"You know me D.W., I'm Jack Feather."

"I like injuns," slurred D.W. as he fell unconscious across the bar, his head hitting with a thud.

"Travis," said Minzo, "I've never seen him this bad."

"I didn't know he was running feral out there", said Travis. "I never even noticed him leave last night. It's a wonder he didn't end up drowned."

"Travis, we got two boys waiting on us down there to go fishing," said Minzo. "Let's put him on the bed in the back room and let him sleep it off. We can run him home right after lunch. Them boys are gonna be mad as wet hornets if we don't get down there real soon."

Travis was only half listening because something had apparently caught his attention out of the window of the Social Club.

"Are those two boys wearing orange life jackets?" asked Travis.

"Yeah, they are, why?"

"Because they aint waiting on you to go fishing no more, look there." Travis pointed out the dirty window.

Minzo raised up on his barstool to look down on the Warrior, where he saw two boys evidently headed for the Gulf of Mexico.

"Son of a gun!" said Minzo. "What the heck has got into them boys?"

Jack and Minzo gave D.W. the bum's rush into the back room and raced for the dock. They jumped into the first boat they saw. Jack manned the oars and began rowing out into the main current of the river. Minzo sat in the stern, a look of bewilderment on his face.

"Son of a buck!" exclaimed Minzo. "Kids nowadays ain't got walking around sense. Thank goodness I made them put their life jackets on. What in the world could they have been thinking? I'm gonna loosen the hide on Donnie's butt when I get my hands on him and Rick's Dad..." Minzo paused in mid-sentence. A concerned look came over his face.

"Jack, would you turn around and tell me what you see out there?" asked Minzo.

Jack was rowing with his back to the action and stopped to look in the direction of the boat. "One of them boys has just jumped into the river!

C hapter 8

"Oh Lord!" moaned Donnie, "My goober's on fire back here."

I turned my attention away from the fish to see Donnie bent over the side of the boat, his pants down, frantically splashing water on his privates.

"What the heck are you doing?" I asked in disbelief.

"I must have got some of that prepper juice on my goober," moaned Donnie.

"Oh man, does that burn. We gotter go back to the dock Rick. I think I may need a doctor. Oh, oooooooh!"

I knew Donnie must have been in real pain because he didn't call me Elmwood. However, I was not about to give up on this fish. The ageless battle of man against nature was more important than a little discomfort.

"Well, you just jump on in and swim back because I'm not about to cut this fish loose."

In Donnie's pain-confused mind, my suggestion to swim back to the dock seemed like a good idea. Uttering not a word he flung himself into the river. Bobbing to the surface, he sighed in relief as the muddy waters of the Warrior cooled the burn. I looked back to see Donnie dog paddling for the Bull Frog and heard Minzo yelling as he and Jack paddled toward us. The disturbance Donnie caused when he jumped in spooked the fish, because it suddenly lunged forward. Mysteriously, it began to circle back toward the Bull Frog and simultaneously began to rise to the surface. I imagined it was growing tired of all this commotion and was heading back to its original hiding place at the dock. I had the feeling that this struggle, for better or worse, was going to end soon.

When the fish broke the surface, I gasped at the countenance of the mighty beast that presented itself. That all too familiar knot began to tighten in my gut from the conflicting feelings of fear and excitement.

This was a catfish of biblical proportions. The creature looked to be six feet long, and its body rippled with cold muscle. Its cavernous mouth opened and closed ominously as it swam, and the huge white whiskers festooning its face gave it the unsettling appearance of a mythological *Medusa*. A dirty white in color, I half expected to see Captain Ahab's lifeless body lashed to the side of the creature. Its sheer size made the chances of actually landing this fish poor at best.

O.K., I thought to myself, *what the heck am I doing! I don't have this fish; it has me!* I was beginning to question whether this was a good idea. But an already tenuous situation was about to take a turn for the worse. I soon realized that the path this fish was taking back to the Bullfrog would very soon overtake one very large piece of bait...Donnie!

"DONNIE!!" I screamed, "DON'T LOOK BACK, JUST SWIM FOR MINZO!"

"Huh?" asked Donnie, turning to look toward me, "What did you....? AHHHHHH!!" Donnie spotted the huge fish swimming directly at him. He began flailing the water furiously as he swam, trying to reach the approaching boat before he became so much stink-bait. The flailing seemed to agitate the fish even more as it began to swim faster.

Donnie was moving water like the Delta Queen, but the fish was still closing the gap. Donnie's progress was being impeded by the bulky life jacket around his neck. He quickly stripped the jacket off and began stroking with renewed fervor. The fish was about to catch up with Donnie when, miraculously, it swam through the looping strap of the life jacket as it floated at the surface. At about the same time, Jack and Minzo arrived on the scene.

"Grab him, Jack," said Minzo as the boat pulled up to Donnie. Jack reached one arm over the side, grabbed him by the shirt collar, and lifted him into the boat. He looked like a drowned rat.

"Alright, boy," said Minzo, "you got a heck of a lot of explaining to do!" Neither Jack nor Minzo had as yet noticed the fish. Donnie, completely out of breath, could only say "Fish! Fish!" while pointing in the direction of the beast.

"What in the world is that?" asked Jack. The fish had now pulled closer to the boat but was swimming considerably slower due to the increased drag caused by the life jacket that completely encircled its head. In addition, it was now impossible for the fish to leave the surface of the water.

"Well that's something you don't see every day!" said Jack, "A white catfish wearing a life jacket."

"Son of a gun," said Minzo, "that boy has done hooked the biggest flathead catfish I have ever seen. Hot dang, we can eat on that fish for a long time." Minzo's anger had vanished like smoke from a hot frying pan.

The fish, still towing me along, passed alongside Minzo and Jack as they watched in amazement from the boat. My arms now ached tremendously.

"Uncle Minzo, help me!" I pleaded as the fish towed me along. "I am just about give out".

"Don't let that son of a gun go. Hang on, boy, we'll get that fish!" said Minzo encouragingly.

"How in the world are we gonna get that fish?" said Minzo under his breath, "That's a big son of a gun."

"No problem," declared Jack, "I'll just grabble it."

Anyone who considered himself a real Riverman grabbled for catfish, although everyone agreed that you had to have a few cards short of a full deck to do it. Grabblers "feel" along the river banks with their bare hands and feet for catfish that they actually catch using only their hands and a length of rope. Requiring a strong back and weak mind, it was not a sport for the squeamish.

"Minzo, take the oars and ease up beside that sucker." Jack cut a piece of stout rope from the boat's bow line and tied a loop in each end. He cinched one loop firmly around the wrist of his left hand. "This'll make sure he don't get away when I grabble him", said Jack confidently. On the other end, he formed a large lasso.

Minzo pulled the boat up alongside the fish, and Jack leaned over to drape the lasso around the fish's head. "Hey, like shooting fish in a barrel," said Jack as he tightened the lasso. I watched from the bow, still clinging to the fishing pole.

In general, fish are not particularly bright, and my experience has led me to believe that catfish are dumber than a sack of hammers. I am convinced that this fish viewed all of the goings-on around him as simply a nuisance and that he never knew he was in any real peril. Until.... he felt that noose tighten around his neck. When Jack leashed himself to that fish, a submarine-launched Trident missile could not have thrown as much water. The rope around Jack's wrist went tight, and he was being shaken like a rag doll in a bulldog's mouth. My arms felt as heavy as spent uranium, and I was actually relieved when the thrashing parted my fishing line.

Although there were a few tense moments, the fish finally tired and Jack prevailed. With Minzo's help, they pulled the fish over into the boat. The creature lay there, its gills and mouth rhythmically opening as it slowly expired. We all marveled at the size of this fish. Its head lay against one seat, and its tail draped up and over the next. It was larger than either of us boys.

While I explained to Minzo and Jack what had happened, we rowed the boats back to the Bull Frog, unloaded the catfish, and hung it from the limb of a large Sycamore tree. Travis fetched his Instamatic Camera, and we all got pictures taken with the fish. Word spread around the fishing camp and the neighboring community, and a small crowd gathered. There was much handshaking and backslapping as everyone congratulated me on an amazing fishing feat. Everyone wanted to hear the story about the white catfish that was caught with a sardine. I tried to explain that Jack had actually landed it, but he would hear nothing of a sort. He wanted me to have all the credit. Later that day, we would weigh the fish, and it would prove to be 93 pounds.

"Son of a gun," said Minzo, "we forgot all about D.W."

Don't worry, I just checked on him, and he is snoring to beat the band in the back room," said Jack. "We can take him home after he sobers up a bit more."

Minzo was sitting, pulling on his chin with his left hand, and staring thoughtfully at the catfish as it hung from the limb of the tree.

"Hmmmm," said Minzo deep in thought. "Jack, I got me an idea on how we could maybe cure D.W. of drinking for good."

"Minzo, the only way to cure D.W. of drinking would be to cut off both his hands, and even then, he would probably take to lapping up whisky like an old tomcat," said Jack.

"You're probably right, but even if this don't cure him, it will at least be a heck of a lot of fun. I'm gonna go inside and give Betty a call."

"What kind of devilment are you hatching in that head of yours?" asked Jack.

"Let me make that phone call and I'll tell you." Jack and Minzo headed for the Social Club, and we were given strict orders to sit in the car and not to get out under any circumstances. A little while later, we saw Mrs. Garrett pull up in D.W.'s pick-up truck. She carried a paper sack and went directly inside. Momentarily, Jack and Minzo came out, untied the fish from its gallows, and lugged it inside.

"What the heck do you think they're doing?" asked Donnie, who had been giving me the silent treatment ever since the burned goober incident. We were hanging out of the windows of the Dirt Dauber, trying to get as good a look as possible.

"I don't know, but they better not mess up my fish."

"Look what's going on now?" Donnie leaned even further out the car window.

Jack and Minzo came out of the Social Club carrying a very large bundle wrapped in bright blue cloth. Mrs. Garrett followed close behind. They all headed for the pick-up truck and loaded the bundle into the driver's side. They then went inside, woke D.W., and carried him out.

"Come on, D.W.," said Minzo, "Betty is waiting for you in the truck." Supporting him under each arm, they escorted him to the truck and placed him in the passenger's seat.

One can only imagine what must have gone through D.W.'s befuddled mind as his eyes focused on what sat in the driver's seat of his pickup truck. Wearing one of Betty's blue sun dresses, bright red lipstick smeared over its cold, slimy lips, pink ribbons tied onto each of those serpentine catfish whiskers, and topped off with one of Betty's straw hats, was the catfish. The sight at first confused, then frightened, and then absolutely terrified as, by God, it spoke in Betty's voice:

"D.W., are you gonna give me a kiss or just sit there?" said Betty, crouching just outside the truck door. D.W. was so agitated that he jumped straight up in his seat in an attempt to get away, hit his head on the truck roof with a loud BONG, and knocked himself out cold. He fell across the seat of the truck.

"Well, I guess we overdid it a little," said Minzo as he and Betty checked on D.W.'s condition. "He's O.K., Betty, just a big knot on his head".

"Minzo, a little bump on the head is nothing compared to all the years of worrying he has caused me," said Betty. "If this cures him of drinking, I will be forever grateful."

Betty drove off down the dusty road. We didn't get to do any more fishing, but spent the rest of the day cleaning and then cooking some of the catfish. Unfortunately, D.W. had no recollection of the entire event and continued drinking unabated. However, from that day forward, he had an unexplainable distaste for fried catfish.

C hapter 9
It seemed the summer of 1962 had gone in a flash, and we were staring another school year in its ugly, pimple-scarred face. Donnie and I had spent as much time as possible with Jack, knowing we would soon be occupied with endless homework, weekend sports, and chores around the house. However, when Jack introduced us to gunpowder, we were so thoroughly intrigued that we vowed to somehow obtain it. The risk of the explosive loss of a body part was overwhelming. But there was one small problem we had to overcome. We had no idea where to get it.

We decided to ask Mrs. Dozier at the Hueytown Public Library. Mrs. Dozier was pretty clueless, and she somehow got the impression that we were researching a class assignment. Probably because that is what Donnie told her we were doing. Nevertheless, we discovered that the components of gunpowder were sulfur, potassium nitrate, and carbon.

"Rick, you got any idear where we can get this stuff?" whispered Donnie as we sat in the reading area of the library.

"We can ask Mr. Allred at the drug store. But what the heck are we gonna tell him why we need it?"

"Don't worry, I'll figure something out," said Donnie.

We hopped on our bikes and pedaled to Allred's Pharmacy, the only drug store in town. We parked our bikes on the sidewalk outside and walked to the Pharmacy counter at the back of the store.

Mr. Allred was a large man, in the neighborhood of 300 pounds. Truthfully, he was so large that he could potentially be in everybody's neighborhood all at once. He was much too short for his weight, with a ruddy complexion, black horn-rimmed glasses, and a white lab coat. He was mostly bald on top, but his curly red hair stuck out from both sides of his head. Whenever I saw him, I always thought of the old joke that goes "What do you get when you cross a so-and-so with a so-and-so?"

He looked like a cross between Humpty Dumpty and an Orangutan. Sitting on a high stool behind the pharmacist's counter, he peered at us over eyeglasses that rode low on his bulbous, red nose.

"What kind of devilment are you boys up to now?" asked Mr. Allred as we approached the counter. Our reputations followed us everywhere we went in Hueytown. I let Donnie do the talking; he was a much better liar.

"Mom sent me to get some medicine for her, Mr. Allred," said Donnie. "Her... uh......pancreatic is bothering her again."

"Her pancreatic? What in the world does that mean?" he asked suspiciously.

"I don't know, but I think that is what she said. It's some kinda female thing," added Donnie. He had overheard his mom use that expression once in discussing a hospital visit.

"Oh, a female thing," said Mr. Allred with a wink.

We had no idea what a female thing meant, but it seemed to satisfy Mr. Allred's curiosity.

"What does she need then?" he asked.

"I wrote it down," said Donnie. He grubbed around in his pants pocket and pulled out a piece of fireball bubble gum and a crumpled wad of paper upon which he had copied the ingredients.

"I'm savin' the bubble grum for a special occrasion," said Donnie with a grin.

Donnie unfolded the wad of paper. "We need, uh....., I mean, she needs sulfer", said Donnie.

"It's on aisle 6."

"She needs some pot-ass-ium ni-tra-te," said Donnie with difficulty. Donnie was a good liar, but his reading skills stank.

"You mean saltpeter," said Mr. Allred. "It's the same thing. It's on aisle 3."

At this point, we were trying not to show our excitement. We had two of the three ingredients that would put us on the road to gunpowder and glory.

"Is that all?" he asked.

"She needs some carbron."

"What is carbron?"

"He means carbon." I corrected.

"Carbon?" said Mr. Allred, his jovial expression changing to suspicion again. "We don't have carbon. Why in the world would she need that?"

"Well... ha, ha... you know that darn female thing," said Donnie.

Mr. Allred didn't seem to buy it this time. "Let's see here, sulfur, salt peter, and carbon. Be sure to tell your mom that if she mixes those things together, she will definitely not have to worry about female trouble again because those are the ingredients for GUNPOWDER!" His voice rose as he spoke the final word.

We were caught. I was stunned. My heart began to race. This old fart knew the ingredients of gunpowder. What were the odds? It was all I could do to keep from bolting from the store. Donnie, the consummate actor, didn't even flinch.

"Grunpowder?" said Donnie innocently. "I'll be sure to tell her that Mr. Allred. I'll bet she didern't know that."

"O.K., boys, run along home. I know what is going on here."

"Mr. Allred," said Donnie, "If mom has to get out of her sick bed to come down for this sturff, she is going to be darn mad at me and at you. You know the kind of fits she can throw."

Indeed, Mrs. Green's fits were legendary. She had been known to rail away, for hours on end, at the most insignificant behavioral infractions. I imagine Mr. Allred must have been considering the unpleasantness of the scene she would create if she had to come into the store, but at the same time, our integrity was at best questionable.

"Give me your phone number," said Mr Allred, as he put the telephone receiver to his ear. "Let's just give your Mom a call."

"Sure thing," said Donnie. "It's Hamilton 5-6540."

Mr. Allred began dialing the number, and I thought Donnie had completely lost his mind. But then he added, "She was asleep when we left the house, and I know she will be really grad to hear from you when you call."

What a stroke of genius that was, I thought.

Mr. Allred paused in mid-dial, gently placed the receiver back on its cradle, and began drumming his fingers on the countertop.

"Well, maybe I shouldn't wake her up then."

He then turned his stare toward me. Somehow, he must have sensed something.

"Rick" he asked, "What are you boys up to? Are you gonna make gunpowder? And don't lie to me boy."

Donnie, trying to cover for me said, "Mr. Allred, now what would we want to make grunpowder for? We aint even got no gruns."

"Hush up, Donnie, I want to hear it from Rick," snapped Mr. Allred.

"Well...? Rick?" said Mr. Allred, staring right at me.

My mind reeled. My stomach knotted. I shuffled my feet nervously. Mr. Allred continued to glare at me. Say something, I thought to myself. Mr. Allred's stare was unbearable. I felt that all of our plans hinged on my response. I felt the pressure building inside me. I opened my mouth to speak...........”BLOOOOOOOOOOOOOOOOOOOOORT”.

A loud fart emanated from my shorts.

I have never been very good at fart control. This has plagued me all of my life. I recall an incident in Mrs. Booth's biology class at Hueytown High. All of Mrs. Booth's lectures were delivered with flawless timing and perfect diction....

"The life cycle of the bladderworm", lectured Mrs. Booth as she stood in the front of the room, "...is a fascinating topic for study." KAPOW. Like an AMEN delivered at a Baptist tent revival, the fart reverberated around the classroom room punctuating her perfectly delivered statement. The class erupted in chaotic peals of laughter. Mrs. Booth was visibly shocked and embarrassed. Students literally fell from their desks onto the floor, holding their sides. Two students were sent to the Principal's Office due to uncontrollable laughing.

And now our carefully laid plans had evaporated like so much swamp gas. Donnie looked at me in disgust. Mr. Allred began to belly laugh uncontrollably. The fat on his neck and jowls jiggled like tapioca pudding. Tears rolled down his fat cheeks, and he was having trouble breathing. Donnie decided that it was all over, headed toward the door and away from the smell. I followed, feeling humiliated and defeated.

"Hold on" said Mr. Allred breathlessly between belly laughs, "Get your sulfur and saltpeter. I'll put it on your Mom's bill. I don't want her to come over and crawl me. But mind you, I will ask her about this the next time I see her, and Rick," he added, "on Aisle 2 you will find the Pepto Bismol." At this, he began to laugh uncontrollably again.

The whole affair had not gone so well, but we did have two of the ingredients that we needed.

"Boy, that was really smooth, Elmword," said Donnie sarcastically as we cycled away.

"Hey, I did that on purpose." An obvious lie.

"Yeah, sure."

Chapter 10

Arguing all the way home, we decided to use my dad's storage shed as our "laboratory." Recalling from biology class that sugar was made primarily of carbon, we decided to substitute that for out missing ingredient. We produced a large quantity of this substance and packed it into sections of aluminum tubing that we had scavenged from an old TV antenna. We fashioned fuses from toilet paper and stuffed them into one end of our homemade rockets. We placed our make-shift rocket on a launching pad, the upturned blade of an old shovel, and aimed it toward the heavens. I lit the fuse and dove for cover behind a gardenia bush where Donnie was already positioned. We counted down in unison.

"Five, four, three, two, one, ignition, blastoff!"

The rocket spluttered and spewed thick, sulfurous smoke. A viscous, black goo oozed out as the propellant slowly burned away.

"Boy, that was whimpy," I said disappointedly. "Donnie, I don't think the sugar was a good idea."

We tried several other "launches" with the same results. Unfortunately, we had used all of our ingredients and produced a large quantity of useless propellant. We grudgingly realized that we did not have the technical expertise to produce quality gunpowder and we simply refused to admit that we did not have enough sense to handle it even if we could. We began to consider alternative sources.

First, we tried stealing my dad's shotgun shells, thinking we could cut them open and remove their contents. However, he kept them locked up in his gun cabinet. Our next idea would prove to be a partial success. It was common knowledge that the local rifle range was also used by the neighborhood police for disposal of confiscated fireworks. Cops would gather by the patrol carloads, build a bonfire, and, amidst an almost party-like atmosphere, would throw cases of the contraband into the consumptive flames. Their private fireworks show. On one occasion, Donnie and I hid in the honeysuckle vines near the rifle range and observed the festivities. If we could not have fireworks, we could at least watch them. We chuckled to see an overweight officer in full uniform carry a box of ordnance to the fire, toss it in, and sort of waddle from the rifle range, stepping ever livelier with each explosion.

To our delight, we discovered, after the police departed, that many of the fireworks were left unexploded. The fuses were burned away, but the powder inside was intact. We now had literally hundreds of cherry bombs and M-80's and each, when cut open, would produce a small quantity of powder.

Donnie and I spent the better part of an afternoon in my dad's storage shed, gathering this material for our rocket. After some time, we had gathered a sizeable pile of powder. We took our arsenal into the backyard.

"Donnie," I asked, "what if this stuff is no good? Maybe the reason these bombs did not go off is that the powder is no good."

"I don't know," said Donnie. "We can always try some."

"Have you got any matches on you?"

"No, all I have is my Dad's Zippo cigarette lighter," said Donnie, "but he don't know I got it and you aint purtting your greasy hands on it cause if it gets messed up he will stomp a mud-hole in my butt."

"Oh come on, Donnie, I aint gonna hurt it. Let me see it just for a minute. I will give it right back. How are we gonna know if this stuff is any good? It was your idea to try some." I prided myself on being able to talk Donnie into almost anything.

"O.K., but don't screw it up," demanded Donnie. He polished it on his t-shirt before handing it to me.

I took the lighter from Donnie and examined it. I understood his concern because this was a beauty of a lighter. It was gold-plated with the insignia of the Coroner's Office on the side.

I separated a small pile of powder from the main stash and pulled it to the edge of the tin plate that it rested upon. A cigarette lighter is great for lighting tobacco products, but it is a poor choice for lighting something lying on the ground. The juxtaposition of the lighter necessitated that my right thumb, unbeknownst to me, was very close to the small volcano of grey powder. I struck the lighter and knelt beside the grey material.

"I'm gonna just light a few particles of powder on the edge of the pile here", I explained as I moved my face closer to ground zero. "I bet this crap is no goo...." KA-WHOOM!

Our entire arsenal went up in a microburst of intense white light and heat. Either due to a simple reflex or the explosive concussion, I was thrown back onto my rear. I inhaled acrid sulfur fumes, and a smell something like roast beef wafted into my nostrils.

"AHHHHHHHH!" I screamed, "I can't see". I was completely blinded by the intense light, and my thumb felt like it had been deep-fried. "Put my thumb out, put my thumb out," I pleaded. Having no visual cues to rely on, I imagined that my thumb was in flames. All I could think of was to plunge my thumb into my mouth to stop the burning.

Donnie had already sprinted to the far side of the yard away from the explosion, but then, realizing the seriousness of the situation, he immediately returned. Obviously concerned for my well-being, Donnie rushed to my side with a terrified look on his face and asked;

"Where's Dad's lighter?"

"Beats the heck out of me, and right now I don't give a flying crap," I said between sucking on my toasted thumb. "I am blinded for life, and you're worried about the stupid lighter."

In the confusion, I had thrown the lighter across the yard, and it had landed in the sandbox. Donnie found it and examined it for damage.

"Oh no," cried Donnie, "look what you did." He cradled the lighter in both hands like a bird with a broken wing. My Dad is gonner krill me," sobbed Donnie.

"Donnie, you idiot, I can't see the darn lighter. I can't see anything."

I have heard that the energy of a nuclear explosion is so great that the silhouettes of those near ground zero can be seen on the walls of the buildings that they stood before- a macabre flash picture taken at the moment of their deaths. I now believe those stories because burned into the side of Uncle Minzo's beautiful Zippo was a perfect silhouette of my thumb. All of the gold plate around the thumb was a hideous grey-green in color. My thumb was also a hideous grey-green.

I never heard if Donnie was punished for ruining his Dad's Zippo. My thumb eventually recovered but my interest in gunpowder did not.

Chapter 11

The phone rang, and Sheriff Jeff Langston, his feet propped on his desk, was startled out of an almost nap. Jeff dropped his feet to the office floor, took the heavy telephone receiver from its cradle, and pressed it to his ear.

"Sheriff's Office," he said in almost reflex fashion. After 25 years on the job, he sometimes even answered his home phone in the same way. Sheriff Langston was probably the largest man in Jefferson County. Standing 6 feet 5 inches in his stocking feet, military style crew cut, and angular facial features, he could have been the poster child for the U.S Marine Corps. Jeff had served an unprecedented 5 terms in office, having never lost an election. However, after 25 years as Sheriff of Jefferson County, the work had become simply the means to a paycheck to support his wife and children. The thrill was gone, and he was not sure he would run for re-election. Still shaking off the mental fog, he did not immediately recognize the voice on the other end of the line.

"Hello Jeff, this is Bob Armstrong." Bob was the mail carrier on the western Jefferson County beat.

"Oh. Hey Bob, how are you?"

"Well, I could be better, but you don't want to hear about that. I'm calling from Howton's Fish Camp. I was just over at Jack Feather's place delivering the mail. You know where it is, up by Lock 17?"

"Oh, sure. I've been there a couple of times. Is there a problem?"

"Well, maybe there is and maybe there isn't. When I delivered the mail this morning, Jack's dogs looked like they hadn't been fed in days. One of them even growled at me like he was sizing me up as a possible meal. On top of that, Jack did not come out to get his mail like he always does. I knocked on the door and called to him, but there was no response. A bad feeling came over me while standing on the porch there."

"It's probably nothing, Bob, but just to be on the safe side, I will take a ride up that way and check it out."

"I would appreciate it. I hope there's nothing wrong."

"Probably nothing to worry about," said Jeff again. "No doubt he's taken another one of his extended fishing trips in that beat-up old boat of his. It's peculiar that he didn't take his dogs, though. At any rate, I will check it out. Thanks for calling. Tell Alice I said hello."

"I'll tell her."

Jeff hung up the phone, took his white, straw, cowboy hat from off the top of a bookshelf, and strapped on his service revolver.

"Martha!" called Jeff, as he headed for the door. "I'm gonna drive over to Lock 17 for a bit. There may be some trouble out at Jack Feather's place. I should be back in about an hour or so."

Martha Sanders had faithfully served Jeff as secretary for all of the 25 years that Jeff had faithfully served the citizens of Jefferson County. Martha was efficient, knowledgeable, and organized. She was at least 250 pounds and had a serious streak of surly in her, particularly in the mornings.

"Don't forget about that meeting with the commissioners this afternoon," said Martha.

"Believe me, I am trying to do just that," said Jeff.

Jeff fired up his patrol car, a 1959 Ford Galaxy, pulled away from the curve, and headed toward the Birmingport Highway. The trip to Jack's only took a few minutes, and soon he was creating a cloud of dust as he drove along the dirt road that led to Jack's house.

Jeff parked in front of the house and got out. The place was quiet, no dogs anywhere to be seen. He noticed that the mail that Bob had placed in the box was uncollected.

He climbed the three steps to the front porch and knocked on the front door.

"Anybody home?!" called Jeff. "Jack? It's Sheriff Langston!"

No sounds came from the house. He noticed that the screen door was latched, but the inner door was slightly ajar. A stiff jerk on the handle popped the simple door latch from the door face. He stuck his head inside the door and called again.

"Jack, you home?"

He stepped into the front room. Nothing out of the ordinary. Worn furniture, stacks of magazines, and newspapers. Apparently, no one at home. Jeff walked to the bedroom and pushed the door open. There was Jack lying on the bed, his arms across his chest.

"Jack. Are you O.K.?........... Oh no!" said Jeff as he placed a hand on Jack's arm and felt nothing but cold flesh.

Jeff pulled the blanket across Jack's face and walked back to his cruiser. Sitting in the front seat, he pulled a stick of gum from his shirt pocket, crammed the stick into his mouth, and tossed the wrapper into the ashtray. His recent decision to stop smoking seemed like a bad idea at that moment. Taking the microphone from its hook, he dialed channel 28 and called headquarters.

"Martha, this is Jeff, have you got your ears on?... Over."

"Come back." replied Martha.

"Martha, call Minzo and tell him to come out to Jack Feather's place as soon as possible, and tell my deputy to get his butt out here also. I'm afraid that Jack has passed away. Over."

A long pause on the radio.

"Martha, are you there?" asked Jeff.

"Yeah, I'm here," said Martha. "That poor man. Does it look like foul play? Over"

"I don't think so. It looks like he passed away in his sleep, very peaceful-like. Over."

"I'll get the coroner out there immediately. Over."

"Thanks", said Jeff, "Over and out."

"Standing by."

By the time Minzo arrived on the scene, Sheriff Langston and Deputy Ray Hines had pretty much wrapped up their investigation, concluding that Jack had passed away from natural causes, although the coroner would have to make the official designation.

"Howdy, Sheriff, Digger." said Minzo, motioning to each.

Everyone called Deputy Ray Hines "Digger" because he dug graves on his days off at the First Methodist Church cemetery. Digger got a cool $25 for every person he planted. Some folks thought it could be a conflict of interest for the Deputy to profit from the dead but Sheriff Langston had never issued Digger a gun. Digger was mostly just a glorified crossing guard.

"What does it look like?" asked Minzo.

"Pretty cut and dry, I think," said Jeff. "Nothing to suggest forced entry, no signs of a struggle, and nothing obviously stolen. Although truthfully, Jack didn't have anything worth stealing."

"I trust it is OK to move the body?" asked Minzo.

"It's all yours," said Jeff.

"Can I get you two to help me carry him out?" asked Minzo. "I need to take him back to the morgue. Given the circumstances, I don't expect an autopsy to be necessary, but we'd better get him into the cooler soon. That'll give me a chance to examine the body more closely."

The three men filed into Jack's broken-down house. They wrapped him in the blanket from his bed and gently carried him to Minzo's waiting station wagon.

"I tell you what, this is a sad thing, him dying out here all alone, and I know two boys who are gonna be heartbroken," said Minzo.

Chapter 12

Mom yelled up the stairwell in the direction of our room, "I am gonna count to three, and if I don't see you kids come down these stairs, I am coming up there with a switch. You ain't too old to get a switching, you know."

"One...two..."

It sounded like a herd of buffalo as my brother and I stampeded downstairs. A confrontation with Mom was definitely the wrong way to begin the new school year.

"You kids finish eating and then get dressed. I want all of you out at that bus stop before 7:00. The buses are running an earlier schedule this year, and so you all are gonna have to start getting up earlier."

Where had the summer gone? I thought as I sleepily pushed oatmeal around in my bowl. It seemed like we had just gotten out of school, and now it was all over. At age 13, I could not imagine anything more depressing than a Monday and the first day of school.

But this summer had been the most remarkable time I had ever spent. Much of my summer had been spent with my best friend Donnie and my newest friend Jack. I hated to see it come to an end.

"Mom," do you think it would be O.K. if I invited Mr. Feather to come to our house for dinner this Sunday after church? He is a really nice man, and this may be the last chance we will have to see him for a while, with school starting and all. You know, we are kind of related to him because he is Cherokee, and Dad said we have some relative that was Cherokee."

"We don't want no dirty Indian coming around here," insisted Frank, my older brother.

"Mr. Feather is not a dirty Indian, and if you don't shut up, you're gonna be wearing this oatmeal on top of your stupid, pumpkin head!" I threatened.

Frank had very red hair, and you could easily rile him by making any reference to that particular feature.

"Oh yeah!" retorted Frank. "How about if I hit you right in the face with this milk? You don't think I'll do it, do you?"

"Alright, that's enough out of both of you," scolded Mom. "Frank, if I ever hear you refer to anyone as "dirty" again, I am gonna wear your butt out with a switch. Do you understand me?"

"Yes Mam," said Frank meekly.

"Rick, if Dad doesn't mind, I don't mind either. Actually, I would like to finally meet this fellow that I've heard so much about. I will ask your father when he gets home today, but I am sure he won't mind," said Mom.

"Thanks, Mom," I said as we headed for the bus stop.

That first school day seemed to drag by. The stifling early September heat made my new school clothes almost unbearable. After a summer of shorts and bare feet, this new ensemble may as well have been a suit of English armor. I was completely miserable. The final class of the day was Math, my least favorite subject. Unfortunately, I had drawn Mrs. Bullock for this class (affectionately known as The Bull). School legend had it that one of her monotonic lectures had driven a 6th grader to throw himself out of an open window into a large holly bush in a misguided attempt to end his suffering. All he succeeded in doing was to give himself a major wedgie and a bad case of "Holly bush rash". Everybody called him "Superboy" after that. The Bull was a no-nonsense, "old school" kind of teacher who believed that fear was the best teacher.

To make matters worse, my seat assignment was front row center. There would be no hiding from The Bull's malevolent gaze.

"How lucky can I get?" I thought to myself sarcastically.

Well, my luck was about to change, unfortunately, for the worse. The seat directly behind me in Biology was occupied by Bobby Sweat. Bobby was one of the biggest cut-ups in junior high. He had been held back in the 4th grade, and combined with his early rush toward maturity, made him at least a head taller than any other kid in class. Bobby was a great guy to be around because he kept everyone in stitches, and his dad was one of the wealthiest men in Hueytown, Alabama. It seemed that Bobby had everything. All the newest toys, a go-cart, a swimming pool, and the great thing about Bobby was that he shared his good fortune with everyone. He did not have a selfish bone in his body.

"Hey, Rick", whispered Bobby close behind me. He leaned low across his desk top, using me as a shield against the eye of The Bull.

"What is it?" I whispered.

"Diarrhea!" whispered Bobby.

To this day, I have no idea why I thought that was so funny. But I tried my best to contain my laughter, I put my hands over my mouth hoping to trap the laughs, but they shot from between my fingers like little devilish imps. Then Bobby began laughing even louder than myself.

Well, I had set a new record. No one in our family had ever been sent to the Principal's Office on the first day of school. But here I was, along with Bobby, sitting in Principal Evans' office, given plenty of time to reflect upon our indiscretions. I think the waiting was the worst thing of all. I imagined all sorts of terrible things that this entry on my "Permanent Record" would cause later in life.

At graduation:

"Congratulations Rick," says the administrator as he hands me my diploma. "Wait a minute here! What's this? There seems to be a problem with your Permanent Record. You don't get a diploma, but we have this nice certificate for you."

Problems in my personal life:

"Louise, will you marry me?" "Yes, oh yes!" says the attractive, black-haired beauty. "OH NO! What is this on your permanent record? Why did you never tell me about this? I can't possibly marry a man sent to the Principal's Office on the first day of school.

The job offers I would never receive:

"Well, Mr. Dodge, you are absolutely our most qualified candidate for this position, and we are prepared to make you a salary offer of

$250,000 per year with full benefits, of course, and... Wait a minute! What's this on your permanent record!? Get out of my office!"

I must say, however, that Principal Evans couldn't have been kinder...kinder like Attila the Hun, kinder like Adolph Hitler, and kinder like Fidel Castro all rolled into one.

"Take your pick, boys..." proclaimed Mr. Evans as he stepped out into his secretary's office, "...after school detention for a week or 5 licks each? But there is one requirement: both of you will take the same punishment. I'll give you a few minutes to decide." Mr. Evans returned to his lair.

"Bobby, we take the paddling. I cannot let my parents know about this, and if I stay after school, there's no way they won't find out".

"No way! My cheeks are still burning from the last time Evans blistered my butt. I vote for detention," said Bobby.

"Bobby, I've got a plan. Trust me on this, and you won't feel a thing when Evans paddles us."

"I don't know...." said Bobby uneasily.

The office door swung open, and Mr. Evans re-entered carrying a three-foot-long, oak paddle, notches carved in the handle for every rear-end it had wounded. We both shuddered at the sight of the weapon he wielded.

"O.K., boys, what will it be?" asked Evans.

"We'll take the paddling!" I quickly replied before Bobby could say anything.

A faint smile crept across the principal's face.

"But sir, could I go to the bathroom first? I gotta pee real bad, and I don't want to have an accident here in the office. Bobby, you need to go to don't you?"

"No, I don't need...."

"Bobby, you really should go because that paddle may find pee you didn't know you had and wouldn't that be embarassin!"

"OK, you're probably right," said Bobby.

"Go ahead," commanded Mr. Evans. "Quickly!"

We hustled down the hall to the boys' restroom.

"Bobby, you dope. You almost messed things up." I chided.

"What did I do?" asked Bobby, confused.

"I don't need to pee. We are gonna stuff our pants full of toilet paper so we won't feel that paddle at all." I explained.

I stepped into the stall, pulled a good quantity of toilet paper off the roll, and put a thick layer of padding between my butt and the principal's paddle. I tried to make it look as inconspicuous as possible.

"Bobby. I'm all set. I'm going back to the office. One thing to remember is that when old man Evan's swats you, be sure to act like it hurts. Do some jigging around and maybe some groaning. But don't overdo it."

"Got it!" said Bobby. He was still in the adjoining stall, preparing his butt armor.

When I got back to the office, Evans was primed and ready. Bobby came in right after me.

"Bend over and grab your ankles," said Evans.

I assumed the position, and Evans let me have it.

Whump! The paddle found its mark. "That's one," said Evans.

"Oooh!" I moaned.

"HA! Didn't feel a thing." I thought. We had pulled this off slicker than owl poop. Evans delivered the remaining four "licks". I stood near the door, rubbing my behind and jumping up and down. An Oscar-winning performance if I must say so. Evans was buying the whole thing.

I watched as Bobby assumed the position. That's when everything fell apart. Bobby had stuffed so much toilet paper into his pants that it looked like he had the rear end of a hippo. In addition, he had left some toilet paper hanging out of the top of his pants.

"Bobby, you have really put on some weight since you went to the restroom," said Evans.

"Huh?" said Bobby.

"Pull all that out of your pants," said Evans. "You boys are about to get on my last nerve. Rick, I knew that paddling didn't feel right. For this little stunt, you will each get an extra lick."

On the bus ride home from school, my butt felt like it had fire ants nesting in it. As soon as I got home, I knew something was wrong. Dad had a very serious look on his face when I met him out in the yard, and he did not want to make eye contact with me. I found Mom sitting in the front room, wringing her hands.

Oh crap! I thought. They must have found out about the paddling. "O.K., let me explain before you explode." I figured it would be best to throw myself at the mercy of the court.

"Explain what?" asked Mom.

"Uh…never mind."

"Sit down, Rick," said Mom. "I have some bad news."

"What's wrong? Did something happen to granddad?" I asked.

"No, your grandfather is fine," said Mom. "Sheriff Langston called this morning. It's Mr. Feather. He passed away in his sleep last night."

"What? I just saw him last week; he was fine."

"I'm so sorry, dear," said Mom.

"No! You're wrong!" I demanded. "I just saw him. I just saw him."

I slammed out of the front door and headed for Jack's on my bike. Pedaling as hard and fast as I could, I arrived at Jack's house in record time. Jack's car was there, but the place was abandoned. Even his dogs were nowhere to be found.

"He's probably on the river in Marie," I thought.

I ran down to find Jack's boat still tied to the cypress tree. I sat on the riverbank, and despite my best efforts to prevent it, tears began to stream down my face. It felt like someone had punched me in the gut. At that moment, it seemed that nothing in the world amounted to much.

Chapter 13
Sheriff Langston pulled up to the Coroner's Office, set the hand brake on his cruiser, and got out. He hated the Coroner's Office. It always had a strange odor, a mixture of formaldehyde, bleach, and cheap cologne that the Sheriff could only stand in small doses. He walked to the door, pushed it open, and was met by Minzo's assistant, Jimmy Payne, who was coming out.

"Oh, hi, Sheriff. Minzo's in the back."

"Hey, Jimmy. Has he finished up yet?"

"Yeah, he finished a little while ago. Looks like natural causes, but I will let Minzo tell you."

Jimmy headed down the sidewalk, and Jeff found his way back to the cold storage area where Minzo was working. Minzo stood over the drawer where Jack's body lay.

"How does it look, Minzo?"

"Hi Jeff. Pretty cut and dry. No marks on the body, no trauma, no evidence of struggle, nothing unusual in the stomach analysis. I'm guessing a heart attack, but definitely natural causes. I really don't see any need to do an autopsy unless you feel differently, Sheriff."

"No. Your opinion is good enough for me," said Jeff. "No use subjecting him to any more indignity than necessary."

"Do you know if Jack had any family?" asked Minzo.

"I don't know for sure, but I believe he was the last member of his tribe of Cherokee. I am pretty sure that he had no remaining relatives at all."

"I don't think he had any money or assets to speak of either," added Jeff. "He has that old car and run-down house and land, but that ain't worth much."

"No money and no relatives," said Minzo. "I guess that means he'll be buried in the cemetery at the State Mental Hospital down in Montgomery."

"Guess so," said Jeff. "Well, at least he will have a good crowd at his funeral. They like for all the patients to attend the funerals just to get them outside for a spell."

"I'll call the folks down at the hospital first thing tomorrow," said Jeff. "How soon do you think you can have the body ready for pickup?"

"I need to finish up some paperwork and then transfer the body to Johnson's Funeral Home. They'll do the embalming. I figure I can have him finished up today, and I'll take him to Johnson's tomorrow. Better give them a day or so. I reckon the day after tomorrow, you can have the hospital folks pick him up."

"That sounds good," said Jeff. "I guess I better call Tom Dodge so he can tell that kid of his. They might want to attend the funeral, such as it is."

"I know Rick and Donnie were good friends with Jack," said Minzo. "Donnie was pretty shaken up when I told him about it. You know, it's a funny thing, but recently, Donnie asked me if Jack could be buried on his property when he died. I don't know where that question came from, but I told him that it shouldn't be a problem. I wish I hadn't said that now. He's gonna be mad at me. I wonder if Jack knew he was dying?"

"I don't know, but with no money, no relatives, and no will, there ain't much anybody could do for him now. The property will go to the state of Alabama, and I am sure they will sell it at auction at some point in the future."

C hapter 14
"They ain't gonner bury Jack on his property," said Donnie.

I had bicycled to Donnie's house to break the news to him about Jack, but Minzo had already told him by the time I got there. We looked out across the barbed wire fence that separated Donnie's yard from the adjacent cow pasture. Donnie was visibly upset, and now I was about to start crying again. I was able to stifle it this time because I wasn't about to cry in front of Donnie.

"Dad said that they were gonner bury Jack in some cemetery in Montgomery," said Donnie dejectedly as he tossed a rock across the cow pasture.

"But I thought Uncle Minzo said that it shouldn't be a problem? Why the heck did he tell you that?"

"I'm telling you that Jack is gonner be taken to Montgomery and buried there," repeated Donnie. "Something about him not having any asserts. Whatever the heck that means."

"We can't let that happen," I demanded; my sadness now turned into indignation. "We told Jack that we would see that he was buried on his property, and we gotta keep our promise."

"What the heck can we do about it?" asked Donnie.

"We gotta take Jack to his house and bury him there. If we can give him a real Indian burial, Jack can come back like he said he would."

"O.K. your starting to creep me out now!" said Donnie. "You don't really believe that do you?"

"No, I don't, but Jack believed it and we made him a promise."

"O.K. how do you plan on doing that? You gonner waltz down to the Coroner's Office and just take Jack?" Donnie picked up a stick from the back yard and began whipping it against the barbed wire fence.

"No, I'm not gonna waltz down there. WE are gonna waltz down there and take Jack," I corrected.

"What!" said Donnie. "Steal Jack from Dad's orffice. You must have your mind rented out!"

"Listen, I've been thinking about this all day. You and I are going to sneak out tonight after everyone goes to bed. We have to do it tonight because you said that Jack was gonna be taken to the funeral home, and that's way across town. I'll get a blanket from the house to wrap Jack in, and you get Ronnie's wagon. We can tie the wagon to the back of the bicycle and use that to carry Jack back to his house. We'll need some rope and a flashlight. I'll get the flashlight; you get the rope. It will be a long ride for us, but if we take turns hauling the wagon, we can get him buried and make it back home before sun-up."

"This is for sure the most hair-brained scheme you have ever come up with," said Donnie, now whipping the fence ever harder. "How are we gonner get into the office when we get there?"

"No problem," I said. "You're gonna steal Minzo's keys."

"Geez-Louise!" Donnie threw his arms into the air in exasperation and tossed his stick into the cow pasture. "How do I get myself inter these things. If Dad frinds out about this, I'll be grounded for life."

"Donnie," I said emphatically, "this is a fool-proof plan. We can do this. We did, after all, promise Jack."

"I guess you are right. But I got a real bad feeling about this."

"O.K. I'll slip out of the house after everyone goes to sleep and come to your house tonight. I reckon that will be around 11:00. You leave your window open so I can get in and wake you up. You got to be sure to get some rope and the keys. DO NOT forget the keys!"

Chapter 15

That evening, everyone was really nice to me at home. Mom cooked my favorite meal, fried chicken, and Dad said that I didn't have to go to school tomorrow if I didn't feel like it. That was completely unheard of around my house. You had to be in a coma to be excused from school. On more than one occasion, when I had tried to feign illness, Mom would pull the same old trick. She would come to my bedside, place her hand on my forehead, and then say, "Oh my! You do have a fever. Let me get dressed, and we're going to see Dr. Carter. But first thing, I am going to give you a dose of *Triple 7*. I can't remember the last time you had a purge."

I would rather be poked, prodded, and stuck with a wagon load of needles the size of railroad spikes than take a single dose of *777 Tonic*. Tonics were commonly given to kids because they were supposed to be good for them. Tonics probably had some health value, but you had to lick a dog's butt to get the taste out of your mouth. All it did for me was make me go to the bathroom about 10 times a day. I don't know what was in that stuff, but if it had one more 7 in it, it would probably just kill you out-right. At any rate, a Triple 7 tonic threat was all it took to snap me out of most illnesses.

After dinner, which I barely touched, I turned in early and lay in my bed, thinking about the events of the day. I had never had such a bad streak of luck in all my 13 years. I could feel the tears welling up again, but I managed to stifle them by thinking about the difficulty of the task at hand. Before sun-up, we would have to break into the Coroner's Office, transport a body in a Western Flyer wagon about 10 miles, perform a Cherokee burial ceremony, and return home unnoticed.

Although I tried to stay awake, I finally fell into a restless sleep.

"Donnie, it's me." I stood outside the open window of Donnie's bedroom, trying to get his attention without waking the entire family.

Standing on tiptoes, I peered in through the window, my head just barely at window-sill level.

"Donnie, wake up," I whispered. "We've got to get going."

In the dim light of the bedroom, I could see a dark shape rising from the bed. Curiously, a pale green fog began pouring across the windowsill and gathered in a swirl at my feet. I could hear a strange, low moaning coming from the bedroom.

"Donnie," I whispered, "be quiet or somebody will hear you."

The moaning stopped, and the dark figure glided effortlessly toward the open window. Suddenly, a decomposed corpse fell across the windowsill, the skull-like head tore away from the body, rolled out the window, and landed at my feet. It opened its ghoulish, green eyes and laughed fiendishly.

"HA, HA, HA, HAAAAA......."

"AAAAAAAAAAH.........." I awoke with a scream and sat straight up in bed. I was breathing hard, and a cold sweat clung to my body. It had only been a dream! I looked at the clock on the wall, and it was almost 11:00. I sat in the dark for a few minutes shivering; the house was deathly quiet, only the sound of my labored breathing. Fortunately, no one had been awakened by my scream.

Having slept in my clothes, I grabbed the flashlight and blanket from under my bed and quietly slipped out of my bedroom window. In a few minutes, I was outside Donnie's window. After my nightmare, the feeling of déjà vu was overwhelming, but looking in the window, I saw Donnie already sitting up in his bed.

"Donnie," I whispered, "it's me."

Donnie came to the window and dropped to the ground beside me. He held a coil of rope in his hand.

"This is really a stupid thing we are doing," whispered Donnie. "I hope you know that."

"Don't worry," I said, "this will be a piece of cake. Did you get Uncle Minzo's keys?"

"Yeah, I got them. But I almost got caught stealing them from his dresser. Ronnie's wagon is under the carport. Let's get this over with!"

We hijacked the wagon, tied one end of the rope to the seat post of my bicycle, and tied the other to the wagon handle. We placed the blanket and flashlight in my bicycle saddlebag. My newspaper route necessitated that I have an extra-large saddle bag to carry papers. I pedaled the bicycle, and Donnie trotted alongside. As we made our way toward Minzo's office, we avoided the main roads and tried to stay away from streetlights, figuring that two kids pulling a wagon with a bicycle might appear suspicious to an onlooker. It took about an hour to arrive at our destination. We decided to go through the alleyway entrance to avoid detection.

"Turn on the flashlight so I can unlock the door," said Donnie softly.

I switched on the light and pointed the beam at the doorknob. Donnie fumbled with the cluster of keys as he tried each one on the ring.

"Crap!" exclaimed Donnie under his breath.

"What's wrong?" I asked.

"None of these keys work on this door," said Donnie.

"Let me try." I jiggled the lock and turned the keys as hard as I dared with no luck.

"This is bad." I declared. "Maybe these keys don't work on the back door. I reckon we'd better go around to the front. But we gotta make it fast. If someone drives by, we'll be up crap creek without a paddle."

Donnie and I crept around to the front entrance. Just as we rounded the corner, the lights from an approaching car illuminated the street.

"Get back!" I whispered. We dove behind a cluster of garbage cans. The patrol car rolled past us and turned down a side street.

"Oh no!" said Donnie. He was visibly shaking. "I think he saw us. We are in so much trouble. We are gonner spend the rest of our rives in jail. What are we gonner do??"

"Donnie!" I had him by the shoulders and was looking him straight in the eye. "Get a hold of yourself. Do you think that cop would have kept going if he had seen us? He'd be all over us like a monkey on a cup-cake."

"Yeah, I gress you are right." Donnie seemed calmer now.

"O.K., let's try the front door. I think the coast is clear."

We tried every key again with no luck. As quickly as possible, we returned to the darkened alley.

"Donnie, you stole the wrong darn keys!!!" I said, very agitated.

"How the heck was I supposed to know which ones to get?" said Donnie defensively. "He's got a whole crap load of them. What the heck do we do now?"

"I'll show you what we do." I wrapped the blanket around my fist, drew back, and smashed my fist into the window next to the rear door. Shattered glass rained down into the alley.

"Oh no!!" groaned Donnie. "We are in deep doo-doo now!"

"It's just a stupid window," I said. "You've broken them before playing ball. What's the difference?"

"The difference is we are gonner be grilty of breaking and entering, destroying pubric property, stealing a bordy, and no telling how many other laws we will break before the night is over."

"So, what's your point?" I said sarcastically.

"The point is we are gonner go to jail for the rest of our lives!"

"Donnie, chill out! We ain't gonna get caught." I reached in through the broken window to unlock the door from the inside.

C hapter 16
Digger Phelps was not happy with his situation at the police department. When he patrolled the late shift, there were plenty of lonesome hours to think about the things that bothered him. And there were lots of things bothering him these days. When he took the job as deputy, he assumed that he would be a full member of the police department, and after four years, he still felt like little more than a security guard. Digger had a temper problem. In his first year on the job, he had pulled his nightstick on a surly teenager and almost killed him. After that, Sheriff Langston kept him on a short leash.

"You screw up one time, and they never forgive you," he thought, his mood darkening. "I always get the crummy jobs. Digger, answer the phone! Digger, sweep up! Digger, wash the patrol car! Digger, go pick up sandwiches! Why doesn't the sheriff trust me?"

Digger turned the patrol car east onto 19th Street and slowly cruised past the storefronts of downtown Bessemer, Alabama. The businesses were locked up for the night, nothing out of the ordinary. Although he was supposed to check each store, he was sick of shaking door knobs. He wasn't gonna get out of his patrol car again tonight unless it was something really important. Digger glanced at the luminous dial on his watch and noted it was 12:05.

"What's the use?" he thought as he turned south on 8th Avenue. "Nothing ever happens in this crummy town."

Digger drove south for a block and then turned down the alley behind City Hall. This was his favorite spot to catch a few winks when he was on night patrol. Driving a short distance up the alley, he switched off the patrol car and settled in for a little snooze. He dozed off for just a moment but was awakened by his full bladder. He got out of the patrol car and relieved himself against a wall. He got back in the car and drove slowly down the alley with his lights off. He did not want anyone to see him emerge from his hiding place. Up ahead, Digger noticed a rear door slightly ajar.

"That don't look right," thought Digger. He got out of the car, walked up the alley, and found an open door and a broken window.

"Dang!" exclaimed Digger quietly. "I think we have us a robbery in progress." Digger hustled back to his patrol car and grabbed his heavy flashlight and night stick. Finally, his big chance to prove to Sheriff Langston that he knew what he was doing. He quietly moved to the open door and paused with his back flat against the wall just outside. Listening intently, he could hear rustling sounds coming from inside the Coroner's Office.

"I should have a dang gun," he thought, unsure of what to do next. His hand shook as he reached for the doorknob, pushed the door slowly open, and stepped into a hallway. It was almost pitch black; dim light filtered in the front window from the street light outside. Digger stopped and listened again. He could clearly hear it now, a rustling coming from the laboratory.

There is someone in there, thought Digger. He was now shaking like a leaf. The last time he got this excited was during hunting season when he was on a deer stand and had a 10-point buck in his gun sights. He shifted the heavy nightstick to his right hand, preparing to smash the skull of the intruder. As Digger approached the door to the lab, the sounds became louder. Digger paused momentarily, took a deep breath to calm himself, and then shouldered through the door into the lab.

"POLICE!" shouted Digger, as he switched on the flashlight and rushed into the room. "You are under arrest."

"YEOWWWW", a big tomcat screamed and rushed across Digger's feet, heading for the alley.

"AHHHHHH!!!" Digger also screamed, threw his nightstick straight up, and fell backwards, landing on his backside. The nightstick fell with a thud on top of Digger's head.

"OHHHHHH!" moaned Digger. He sat for a moment trying to figure out what had just happened. He got up and found the overhead light switch. Turning it on, he found no one else in the room.

"Stupid cat!" mumbled Digger, as he rubbed the growing lump on top of his head. Digger looked around the lab and realized that something was indeed not right. One of the large drawers that was used to store bodies was pulled open, and there was no body inside! Digger checked the name on the drawer end.

"Jack Feather," read Digger out loud. "Somebody took Jack. Why in heck would somebody steal Jack's body?"

Digger was beginning to feel better now. The throbbing in his head had subsided somewhat, and he didn't feel quite so stupid. He had never before been the first investigator at a crime scene, and this crime scene he had all to himself. There wasn't much to investigate, however. He figured it must have happened within the last few hours because he had cruised this alley earlier and was certain that nothing was amiss. Digger went outside to the patrol car, reached in through the passenger's window, and switched on the CB radio. He removed the microphone from its hook and dialed in the channel that Sheriff Langston monitored at his home. Digger paused, reached back in the window, and placed the microphone back on its hook.

"To heck with this," thought Digger. "I'm going to solve this case myself before sun-up. That'll prove to Langston that I'm not a screwup. But I ain't about to do this without a gun."

Digger headed for the Police Station. He would requisition himself a pistol and then heaven help the body snatchers when he caught up with them.

Chapter 17

"Stop!" commanded Donnie as he fell to his knees on the dirty pavement. We had wrapped Jack in a blanket and secured him in the wagon. I was pumping my heart out on the bicycle, trying to put as much distance as possible between us and Minzo's Office. Donnie had been running alongside and was pretty much winded.

"Let me ride the bike a while," said Donnie between gasps. "I feel like I'm about to throw up."

"No problem." I got off the bike and let Donnie take it. "Did you hear something right after we left Minzo's Office?"

"I didn't hear anything," said Donnie as he climbed on the bicycle.

"I swear I thought I heard a noise from inside Minzo's Office. I guess I was just imagining things."

Despite the little problem with the keys, our plan was on schedule. We were making good time in the direction of Jack's house, and if all went well, we would have Jack safely buried well before sun-up.

"Donnie," I said. "We need to get off the street as soon as we can. It makes me nervous to be out in the open like this."

"Works for me," said Donnie. "We can take the shortcut across Fart-Man's Squeeze and then through old man Walker's junk yard. We'll come out on Birmingport Highway, and then we just have to follow the highway to the Warrior River and Jack's house."

"You mean Fat-Man's Squeeze."

"That's what I said, Fart-Man's Squeeze."

"I don't know. Do you think we can get this wagon through The Squeeze?"

"No probreem-O."

"O.K., let's go."

We headed out along the horse trails that led to Fat Man's Squeeze. The "squeeze" was a small canyon on the outskirts of town, aptly named for its narrow stone passages. The horse trails emerged at the top of the canyon, and to get through, we would have to climb down into it through some of the narrowest and steepest "squeezes". We stumbled through the darkened forest, saving the flashlight batteries for later. Donnie was in the lead, pushing the bike, and I was pulling the wagon containing Jack.

"Man, it's darker than the inside of a cow!" said Donnie as he walked headlong into a huge spider web that enveloped his face.

"AAAAAAAAH!!!" screamed Donnie, "GET IT OFF! GET IT OFF! AAAAAAAH!"

Donnie was royally freaking out, beating his head and face.

"What is it?" I asked, not realizing what was upsetting him.

"SPIDER! SPIDER!" yelled Donnie.

I grabbed the flashlight and switched it on. Giving Donnie a quick inspection, I found nothing.

"Calm down Donnie. There's nothing on you."

"Man, I hate spiders!" said Donnie as he stood there shuddering.

We continued walking, this time with the flashlight on. Donnie pulled out his harmonica and began playing "Sweet Georgia Brown". We were soon at the top of the canyon.

"Watch out!" said Donnie as he pointed the flashlight over the edge of the canyon. "One slip here and you'll be nothing but a greasy spot down at the bottom."

"Do I look like an idiot? Don't answer that! Let's find the path leading down into the canyon." I added. "I think it's over this way."

I took one wrong step and found myself teetering on the edge of the canyon. "Whoaaaaaaaaaa!" Donnie grabbed me by my t-shirt and pulled me back from the edge.

"Whew, that was close," I said, relieved. "Why don't you go first?"

Using the flashlight, we moved carefully along the edge of the canyon searching for the path that led down. The search took longer than we had anticipated, but we finally found the narrow notch at the top of the canyon.

"Here it is!" said Donnie. "I was starting to think we weren't going to find it."

"Man, I don't think the wagon is gonna fit down that path."

"Sure it will," replied Donnie. "We'll leave the bike and Jack up here and take the wagon down first. We'll carry Jack down afterwards."

"O.K., let's give it a try."

I pulled the wagon to the top of the path and started down. Donnie was bringing up the rear. We had gone barely five steps when the wagon jammed between the stone walls of the trail. Despite my efforts, it would not budge.

"GREAT!!!" I declared disgustedly. "This thing is stuck tighter than a tick on a dog's butt. Donnie, on the count of three, you push real hard on the back while I pull."

"One, two, three...push!"

Donnie gave the wagon a heave, and I pulled my heart out.

"Keep pushing, Donnie, I think it's......."

Suddenly, the wagon broke loose and took off like a rodeo bull coming out of the gate. Donnie fell face down in the trail, and I toppled into the wagon as it careened down the canyon trail heading for certain destruction.

"HELLLLLLLLP," I screamed. My plea trailed off as I descended into the dark canyon.

The wagon ricocheted off the granite walls, throwing sparks with each collision, and throwing me against the stony walls of the trail. Between collisions, I somehow managed to turn around in the wagon and grab the handle to attempt to steer. Unfortunately, the banana spiders had been hard at work this night, and the trail was strung with a seemingly endless supply of webs. All of the webs seemed to be at just about face level. I was steering with one hand, trying to wipe sticky web and spiders from my face with the other, and screaming all the while. Near the bottom of the canyon, the wagon finally went airborne as it flew over a ledge and landed in the creek.

"AHHHHHHHH!!"

The water was only a few feet deep, but it was enough to break my fall. I sat in the cold water for a few minutes, trying to catch my breath and examining myself for serious injury. Donnie came running down the trail and found me perched in the wagon in the shallow creek.

"Man!" said Donnie excitedly. "That was so cool. Did you see those sparks? You looked like a rocket ship taking off. Let me do it."

"Shut up, Donnie," I demanded, rising from the wagon slowly. "That could have killed me!"

"Hey, you're OK, aren't you?"

"Yeah, I'm just fine and dandy!" I answered sarcastically. "Let's go back up and get Jack. I want to get the heck out of here."

We hiked back up to the trailhead and found the bike and Jack just as we had left them.

"You take Jack, and I'll take the bike down."

"I got a better idea," said Donnie. I'll take the bike, and you take Jack. Man, it really creeps me out to touch him, you know, now that he is dead and all."

"O.K., we will both take Jack down and then come back for the bike."

We walked over to Jack and bent over to pick him up. We both came face to face with a very large cottonmouth snake coiled on the body closer to Donnie's end. We simultaneously jumped back as the cottonmouth struck at Donnie, but found only thin air. The snake slithered from Jack's body and slowly crawled into the underbrush

"Holy cow!" said Donnie. "I bretter check my britches because I berieve I've done soiled my underprants."

"Now you know how I felt when I took that ride down into the canyon."

"You think this is some kind of Cherokee sign or something?" asked Donnie. "Maybe we shouldn't be doing this. Maybe the spirits are trying to tell us something. Maybe that srake was one of Jack's relatives trying to warn us."

"Donnie, will you shut up! Jack asked us to do this, and we promised to do it. End of story!"

C hapter 18
We moved quickly through the remainder of the canyon and emerged from the woods near a small group of house trailers across the street from Walker's Junk Yard. Walkers was the largest junk yard in north Alabama, maybe in the entire state. It ran for many blocks along Highway 24. To the east of the junk yard was The U.S. Pipe Shop, and to the west was The Tennessee, Coal and Iron Corporation, both of which were surrounded by high fencing with barbed wire, security lighting, and guards. The low fence of the junk yard made it the easiest and quickest route to the Warrior River. Plus, the junk yard was cris-crossed with fairly smooth access roads that would make hauling Jack's body much easier. We figured the yard would be abandoned at this hour, so there should be little chance of being detected.

We paused on the other side of the road near the trailer park before making our run across to the junk yard. Most of the trailers were dark at this hour, the exception being the one nearest the highway with the garishly lit "Madam Lavonia Monet, Palm Reader" sign out front. We had all heard about Madam Lavonia, but most folks stayed away from her trailer because it was said that she was stark raving mad.

"Man, I am thirsty. We should have brought some water."

"Me too," agreed Donnie. "I'm about as dry as a popcorn fart. Why don't you go up to Madam Lavronia's and see if she will give us a drink of warter? All the rights are on in her trailer, so she must still be awake."

"I don't know." I wasn't sure this was a good idea. "Let's both go up there. We'll leave Jack hidden here, and we can tell her we are camping out back at Fat Man's Squeeze. I could use a big glass of lemonade right now."

"Man, that would be good," agreed Donnie, scratching his chin, obviously weighing the pros and cons of this move. "O.K., let's do it."

We made sure Jack was safe and walked over to Lavonia's. The lights were on throughout the house, and music wafted through the open front windows. We could hear Lavonia singing "You are my sunshine" from somewhere in the house. We knocked, the singing stopped, and she came to the front door. Lavonia looked to be in her late 60s. She was dressed in a long white gown, house-slippers, and had a pale blue cloth wrapped around her head like a swami. Her cheeks were heavily rouged, and she wore too much lipstick that was too red. She reminded me of my grandmother, minus the make-up.

"What the heck are you boys doing out at this time of night?" asked Lavonia.

"Sorry to bother you so late, Ma'am," I said. "We are camping out in the woods back there, and we forgot to bring anything to drink. Would you mind giving us a glass of water or whatever you have?" I was hoping for a Coke or maybe some lemonade.

"Aren't you Minzo Jones' son?" asked Lavonia, looking at Donnie.

"Yes, Mam."

"Y'all come on in and sit down. I've got some root beer and Cokes in the ice box, or I can get you some ice water if that's what you want."

"I'll take a root beer," said Donnie.

"Me too."

I had never been to a Palm Reader before, and the front room of the trailer took me by surprise. The walls were covered with purple, crushed velvet wallpaper. Candles were set on stands all around the room. There was a sculpture of a human eye, about two feet across, staring out at us, that hung from the wall just behind a velvet-covered "reading table". On the reading table was a pale blue crystal ball sitting upon a black base. This was where Lavonia did her fortune telling, card reading, and palm reading. She could tell that we were both very much impressed.

"You boys sit at the table there, and I'll bring you your root beers. You can look all you want, but don't touch anything on the table. O.K.?"

"Yes, ma'am," we both said.

"Man, this place is brootiful," said Donnie. "Look at all this stuff."

Donnie reached out to grab a deck of weird looking cards that lay on the table.

"Don't touch those," I demanded. "Didn't you hear what Lavonia just said?"

"O.K., O.K.!" said Donnie, perturbed. "Hey, let's ask her to give us a reading? It'll be fun."

"We don't got no money. See that sign on the wall over there."

The sign read "Palm Reading- $10.00, Tarot Card Reading- $10.00, Communication with The Deceased- $15.00, All Three- $30.00.

"Maybe she will do it for free. She ain't got anythring else to do. It'll be sort of like practice for her. Maybe she can talk to Jack."

"Shut up! Don't kid around about Jack."

"Sorry," said Donnie apologetically.

Lavonia returned and handed us each a root beer and placed a bowl of parched peanuts on the table in front of us. "I thought you might like some of these goobers. I roasted them today. Just don't get shells all over the place."

Lavonia sat down across from us, picked up her deck of cards, and began shuffling them. She dealt 3 cards face down on the red velour tablecloth.

"Your turbrin is brootiful," said Donnie between swallows of root beer.

"My what is what?" asked Lavonia.

"He said your turban is beautiful."

"Isn't that what I just said?" questioned Donnie, agitation in his voice.

"Whatever."

"Are you gonner tell our fortunes?" asked Donnie.

"I can't tell fortunes. I can use these cards to provide some clues about events that might happen in the future. But there ain't no guarantee about anything. Your future is determined by the choices you make in the present."

"Cool!" said Donnie. "Can you tralk to dead people, because my dad knows lots of dead people that he would like to tralk to. Well, he doesn't know them now because they are dead, but he knew them before they were dead. Well, he didn't know all of them, but he had to try to figure out how they got dead and..."

"Donnie, would you shut up!" I said, giving him a mean look.

"I'll shut up," said Donnie sheepishly.

"Let's just do a card reading and see what we get," said Lavonia. She got up, lit several candles, and then turned the lights off. "I have to have the right atmosphere. I also need you to be absolutely quiet while I do my reading. It takes great concentration."

The flickering candles cast weird shadows that pulsed across the walls and Lavonia's face as she took her seat at the table. The only sounds were Donnie and me slurping root beer and munching peanuts. Lavonia turned the first card face up. The card depicted a funny-looking person dressed in colorful, garish clothing.

"Hmmmm," said Lavonia. "Very interesting!" She had our complete attention.

"What is it? What do you see?" said Donnie, apparently about to explode.

"This is "The Fool". This card indicates a beginning. Most probably a journey, either physical, mental, or spiritual. It can mean unexpected happenings or important decisions to be made. Are you boys going on a trip somewhere soon?"

"No, not us." We both answered.

Lavonia turned over the next card. There was a knight in black armor astride a white horse.

"This is the Death card," she said.

Donnie and I both gasped simultaneously. We must have had pained looks on our faces.

"Don't look so worried, boys," said Lavonia. "It doesn't necessarily mean physical death. It can mean a major change in your life, a new beginning, the end of one life phase, and the beginning of another. It doesn't have to mean something bad."

"Finally," said Lavonia, as she reached for the third card. "The last card is the most important. It has the greatest influence on future events." Lavonia turned the card over to reveal "The Devil". Despite the heavy makeup, the color drained from Lavonia's face. Just at that moment, we heard a dog snarling and barking wildly nearby, a car sped along the highway, and the wind picked up and whistled around the trailer.

"This reading is over, boys," announced Lavonia.

"Wha...wha...what did you see?" stuttered Donnie.

"Nothing," said Lavonia as she gathered up all of her cards, rose from her seat, and turned the room lights back on. "I want you boys to be really careful tonight while camping. There's been some strange stuff going on around here. As a matter of fact, why don't you boys just stay here with me tonight? I can call Minzo and let him know that you are gonna be here. I'll tell him you just got spooked out there in those woods and came to my trailer. I know him well and that..."

"We really appreciate the offer, Ma'am, but we better get back to our campsite," I said as I quickly got up from the table. "Thanks for the drinks and peanuts."

"Did you see something bad?" Asked Donnie.

"Let's go, Donnie!" I demanded as I hustled him out of the trailer.

"Listen, boys," said Lavonia from the door of the trailer. "If you need anything, I will be right here."

"Thank you!" I called as we hurried toward the woods.

"I am going home!" announced Donnie as he stomped around the darkened clearing. "Why did I let you talk me into this crazy groose chase?"

"Wild goose chase." I corrected.

"Whatever!" shouted Donnie. "I'm almost killed by the most poisonous snake in the world, you won't let me ride the wagon, we broke into Dad's orffice. Did you hear what she said? She knew we were on a journey and that last card had "The Devil" written on it. I saw it when she turned it over. Did you see the look on her face when she saw that card? That was a bad card. She knows that something bad is gonner happen. Oh man. This is sooo bad."

"Are you finished?" I asked.

"What?" asked Donnie, throwing his arms straight out for dramatic emphasis. "Am I the only one that sees the probrem here?"

"Dad-blame it, Donnie," I said disgustedly, "I knew it was a bad idea to go in there. You don't actually believe that stuff, do you?"

"Well, how did she know those things?" asked Donnie.

"She didn't KNOW anything. All she said was something about a journey and a new beginning. And maybe what she saw wasn't something bad happening to us, but maybe it was Jack? Maybe she knew that we were taking his body somewhere. Did you ever think about that?"

"I guess," admitted Donnie.

"The best thing for us to do is to get across that junk yard and get Jack buried. We don't have much further to go."

"I guess you're right."

"O.K. Let's get out of here."

Crossing the fence into Walker's junk yard was a breeze. We hefted the bicycle, wagon, and Jack over a low place in the fence and climbed over. There was a full moon, so there was plenty of light. The deep shadows cast by the piles of junked cars made the place feel like a graveyard instead of a junkyard. And I guess it was kind of a graveyard...for cars. We hooked the wagon to the bike and loaded Jack back into it. Donnie pedaled the bicycle while I pushed from the rear. The weight of moving countless junked cars through the yard created a hard-packed surface that made travel fairly easy. We were both unaware that a major obstacle lay in our path through this ghostly auto graveyard. That obstacle was Mr. Walker's German Shepherd "Fang".

Fang was the meanest German shepherd anyone in these parts had ever seen. Rumor had it that this dog was directly descended from the Canine Corps that guarded Hitler's secret bunker. I had first-hand experience with the evil Fang. Most of us kids had a newspaper route, and Mr. Walker's home was on mine. All summer long, I had a running battle with this dog. Actually, there was little battle to it. Fang would chase me, snarling, and I would frantically try to get away. Whether I tried to sneak by slowly or whiz by fast, he would bolt out from some bush or other and harass me, snapping and lunging for several blocks.

Recently, Mr. Walker had moved Fang from his home to the junkyard because thieves had been stripping car parts after dark. He knew that no car parts would be stolen with Fang on duty. Donnie and I were not aware that we were now on a collision course with the dog from Hades.

"This place is definitely spooky," I whispered.

"Do you think there is anyone here?"

"I doubt it. But just in case, let's stay in the shadows as much as possible."

We stuck close to the huge piles of junk cars and slowly progressed across the yard. We could see the fence on the far side of the yard in the moonlit distance.

"We're almrost there," said Donnie. "Just a little farther."

"Yeah. Not much further......OOOOF." I tripped and fell across the end of an old car fender. The fender sprang up with a loud CLANG! That's when we heard the barking. It was a low, thunderous bark that came from somewhere behind us. We had not been aware of it, but we had passed by the sleeping Fang. But now he was awake, he had our scent, and he was approaching like a heat-seeking missile.

"What the heck is that?" asked Donnie.

"I don't know, but pedal like mad cause it's coming this way."

"Oh no! Oh no! Oh no!" cried Donnie as he began pedaling the bike as fast as he could. I pushed like crazy on the back of the wagon, hoping to make it to the safety of the fence. We hadn't gone 20 feet when the shadowy figure of Fang streaked into view behind us.

C hapter 19

Digger felt empowered. He caressed the cold steel of the revolver that lay on the seat next to him as he cruised the streets of Bessemer. He had loaded the gun with six hollow-point cartridges. Although he had never actually fired a service revolver, he figured that it couldn't be much different from firing a rifle.

"Digger, have you got your ears on?" Sheriff Langdon's voice crackled over the police radio.

"Oh crap!" thought Digger. He must have found out about the break-in at the Coroner's Office. Digger reluctantly pulled the microphone from its hook.

"This is Deputy Phelps. Over.", said Digger nervously.

"I just got a phone call from Lavonia Miller. She said that two kids were over at her trailer on Highway 24. They said they were camping out near Fat Man's Squeeze, and asked her for some water. She said they were acting kind of strange. I don't know what she meant by that, but drive over there and check it out. It's probably nothing, but it will make her feel better if you cruise by. Over."

"I'll cruise over there right now. Over," said Digger, relieved.

"See if you can locate the boys while you are over there. If they are camping, it should be fairly easy to find them. Let me know when you do. Those boys shouldn't be wandering around at this time of night. Over."

"Ten-four," said Digger. "Over and out". *The story of my life. Nurse maid to a loony old lady and a couple of bratty kids.*

Digger pulled his cruiser onto 9th street and headed north toward Madam Lavonia's. In less than 15 minutes, he was parking his car on the side of Highway 24 in front of her trailer. Digger got out, scanned the woods behind Lavonia's to see if he could spot a campfire, and then knocked on Lavonia's door.

"Hi, Mrs. Miller," said Digger as she appeared.

"Hello Digger."

"Sheriff radioed and asked me to cruise over here. Said something about two boys."

"They left about 20 minutes ago. Headed toward the woods back there. They were acting nervous, like something was going on. I just got this feeling that they were up to something."

"I'll walk around and see if I can locate them if that will make you feel better."

"Thanks. If you find them, I want you to load 'em up and take 'em home. I don't want those kids starting a forest fire back in those woods. It's been awfully dry lately, and this old trailer would go up like a box of matches."

Lavonia hoped this story would convince Digger to find them and take them home. She was very upset and afraid for the boys. When she had turned over the "Devil" card during that reading, she just knew that something bad was going to happen.

"Yes, ma'am. I'll see if I can locate them, and I'll take them both home."

Digger went to his cruiser and reached in to retrieve his flashlight. He also grabbed the revolver and slipped it into his pants pocket. He wasn't fond of walking around in the woods at night, and the gun gave him more confidence than he deserved. He walked a short distance down the road, paralleling the fence that ran along Walker's Junk Yard. He was about to enter the woods when he heard the barking.

"What the heck is going on over there?" Digger thought as he crossed the road toward the junkyard. He walked to the office and checked the door and the gate. Both were locked. The gap between the gate and the fence post was wide, and, being skinny, Digger was pretty sure he could slip through. He hesitated, afraid of what he might find inside. He placed his hand in his pocket and felt the revolver. Digger quietly slipped through the fence and, gun drawn, nervously walked toward the barking.

C hapter 20
"We ain't gonner make it," cried Donnie. He leapt from the bike and took off on foot. I was soon running right behind him, but we had clearly lost too much time to beat Fang to the safety of the fence.

"Quick," I said breathlessly. "Climb on top of the junk pile."

As far as we were concerned, it was a matter of life and death, and we climbed like demons were after us. Donnie beat me to the top of the pile. At the last moment, Fang leapt and grabbed me by the heel of my tennis shoe. He began shaking it like a rag doll, using his weight to pull me from my perch.

"Donnie, help me!" I pleaded.

Donnie grabbed me by the arm.

"PULL DONNIE, PULL!' I was begging for him to save me from the jaws of Fang. Donnie pulled, and Fang came completely off the ground, suspended by my skinny leg. I thought he was gonna rip my leg off when, fortunately, my tennis shoe pulled off, and Fang crashed to the ground at the base of the junk pile.

"Holy Cow!!" I said, almost in tears. "I thought I was dead. You saved my life."

We were lying on the roof of a junk Mercury Comet that was stacked on top of two other junk cars, pretty sure that Fang could not reach us. We were both panting hard and sweating like pigs. We cautiously peered over the edge to see Fang occupied with trying to eat my tennis shoe, snarling, dog slobber flying everywhere.

"Well, at least he's not eating Jack," said Donnie.

Suddenly, Fang stopped and looked back toward the front gate. He took off like a shot, barking like a banshee.

"What's gotten into him now?" asked Donnie.

"Who knows what that crazy sack of evil is up to?" He must have smelled something. Maybe a coon or possum. I don't care what it is, I'm just glad he's gone."

Digger paused and listened. The barking had stopped, and now he wasn't sure of which way to go. In the dark, the piles of junked cars all looked alike. He was also not sure he could find his way back out again. He stood in the shadow of a junk pile, wondering what to do next, when the barking started again. It was definitely coming from the direction of the back fence. But then he realized that the sound was getting louder. Whatever was making all the noise was definitely coming towards him. Digger pulled the hammer back on his revolver. Just at that moment, Digger spotted a large snarling dog coming around the corner of a junk pile, running at full speed.

"Oh crap!" cried Digger as he pointed the pistol at the oncoming canine.

Fang heard Digger's exclamation, which infuriated the dog even more. Digger backed away as the dog approached and squeezed off two shots in rapid succession. One bullet hit the ground 20 feet in front of the dog, and the other one went wide and hit a junked car in the door with a loud KAWANG! The gunfire did nothing to slow the dog, and it lunged at Digger.

"Oh my lord," moaned Digger. Acting on reflex, he pointed the gun at the dog and pulled the trigger. Fang fell to the ground howling, kicked violently, and died.

"Stupid, worthless mutt," said Digger, breathing hard. "He won't be messing with anybody else now."

Digger was now quite unsure of which way to go to get out of this maze. The many piles of junked cars made navigating very confusing.

I think the gate is this way. He didn't know it, but he was heading straight for the back fence.

C hapter 21
"What was that?" whispered Donnie.

"Dang! That was gunfire!" I said under my breath. "And it sounded close. Who the heck is shooting a gun at this time of night?"

"That sounds like Fang howling," said Donnie. "Somebody just shot that lunatic dorg."

"This ain't good, this definitely ain't good," I whispered. "Donnie, let's get our skinny butts out of here as fast as possible. If we can get over that back fence, we'll be in the clear."

"Heck no!" said Donnie. "Let's wait up here until we know the coast is clear."

"Or until whoever that was that just shot Fang comes and shoots us?" I retorted. "You can stay, but I'm out of here."

I was fast getting a gut-full of Donnie, and this adventure had long ago lost its luster. Just as I was about to climb down, Donnie spotted a shadowy figure coming across the junk yard.

"Rick, somebody's coming," whispered Donnie.

We flattened ourselves against the roof of the junked car we lay upon.

When Digger spotted the rear fence of the junk yard, he realized that he was walking the wrong way.

"Oh crap," thought Digger when he realized his mistake. He looked around nervously. He was on edge after the encounter he had with the crazed dog. Digger turned to walk in the opposite direction when he stumbled upon a large object. He pulled his flashlight out to investigate.

"What the heck is this?" muttered Digger. Using the toe of his boot, he pulled the blanket back. That's when he saw the lifeless, ashen face of Jack Feather. "What the Hell??" Jack's face took him completely by surprise. Digger jumped away from the corpse as a cold chill crept through him.

Donnie and I watched as the mysterious figure stooped over the lifeless body.

"Oh no!" I whispered nervously. "He found Jack."

"I've got an idea," said Donnie.

"Grrrrrrrrrrrrrrrr," Donnie began to make a low growling sound.

"Donnie," I whispered "Are you nuts, he's gonna hear you."

"That's whart I want him to do. Grrrrrrrrrrrrrrr," Donnie growled even louder and punctuated it with a pretty convincing, guttural bark.

We watched the intruder's reaction from the safety of our hiding place.

Digger pulled the revolver from his pocket and nervously pointed it and his flashlight all around, reacting to every sound around him. In the dark, he could not tell where the sound was coming from, but he was sure there was some other animal nearby. This was too much for Digger, and he immediately took off running as fast as he could go.

"It worked," said Donnie triumphantly.

"Let's get out of here!" I whispered to Donnie.

I climbed down from the junk pile and located my slobbery shoe. We grabbed the bike and Jack, and we headed for the back fence. Finding a gap between the bottom of the fence and the ground, we pulled Jack, the bike, and the wagon through as quickly and quietly as possible. We stopped on the railroad tracks that were just outside the fence to collect our thoughts. Donnie sat down on the rails and opened his mouth to speak.

"Don't even say it, Donnie!" I was obviously agitated. "We are in too deep, and there is no way we can back out of this now."

"All I was gonner say..." said Donnie defensively, "was that we need to get far away from here. Do you know where these tracks go?"

"I'm pretty sure they go into the steel mills in that direction," I pointed down the tracks, "and to Birmingport in that direction. I think I remember Dad talking about the train hauling iron ore into the steel plant."

"If the tracks go to Birmingport we can follow them right to the river," said Donnie. "Then we just follow the riverbank downstream to Jack's place."

"Donnie! Listen. Do you hear that!"

In the distance, we could hear a low roaring sound that was getting louder, and way off down the tracks, we could see the light of an approaching train.

"We better get off'er these tracks," said Donnie. "We don't want that train running us over."

"Wait a minute. I think I got an idea. The train has to slow down for that road crossing up ahead, don't it?

"I guess so," said Donnie suspiciously. "I don't know if I like this idea."

"If he slows down enough, we can load Jack into one of the box cars if the door is open. We can get to the river crossing a lot faster that way. When it slows down again at the Warrior River bridge, we can just get off agin."

"What if it don't slow down?" asked Donnie.

"If he doesn't slow up, we'll just have to walk to the river. Let's get up to that road crossing."

We high-tailed it to the road crossing well ahead of the train. We hid Jack, the bike, and the wagon in the undergrowth near the track as close as we dared without risking detection. Donnie and I sat in the brush near the track's edge. Donnie took his harmonica from his pocket and began to softly play Chattanooga Choo Choo. With a little luck, this would cut at least an hour off our trip.

C hapter 22
As the train approached, it was obvious that it was traveling much too fast for us to get on board. We sat and watched dozens of cars rumble by, assuming that we wouldn't be taking any train trip tonight, when suddenly the train began to slow.

"Get ready, Donnie," I had to yell over the rattle and clang.

Miraculously, the train came to a complete stop with an open boxcar right in front of us.

"Let's go!"

We sprinted to where Jack was hidden and pulled him to the open door. We had to lift him several feet off the ground, which would have been impossible had the train been moving. It took all of our strength to get him into the car.

"Let's get the bike and wagorn," said Donnie as we ran back toward the underbrush.

Donnie had his harmonica in his hand and, for some screwy reason, put it back in his mouth. He started playing Chattanooga Choo Choo again.

No sooner had we left the track-side when there was a series of loud clangs and a lurch, and the train began to move again. I had freed the bike from the undergrowth, and Donnie was struggling to free the wagon from the honeysuckle vines that had entangled it.

"Donnie! The train is moving. Forget the wagon."

Donnie was furiously jerking on the wagon and playing very fast-paced. I threw my bike down and went over to help free it. I looked over my shoulder to see the train moving faster now.

"Donnie, it's no use," I said. "If we don't get on that train fast, Jack's gonna be really mad at us."

Donnie stopped jerking on the wagon and gave me a really odd look. He continued playing.

"Sorry about that. I got carried away."

We abandoned both the wagon and the bike and ran for the train that was now moving faster. The roar of all that metal in motion was deafening. We ran alongside the train, preparing to jump on board.

"Donnie," I yelled breathlessly as we jogged along the track. "Which one of these cars has Jack in it? They all look alike."

"I think it's that yellow, rusty one just ahead," yelled Donnie between harmonica notes.

We ran up to the next car and tried to peer in as we ran along. Jack was obviously not there. The train lurched again and picked up even more speed. We were now having trouble staying up.

"Faster, Donnie, faster," I yelled. We were now running about as fast as we could go and realized that we would have to jump into the next car. I could hear breathy harmonica notes right on my heels, so I knew Donnie was there. We would just have to hope that we had picked the correct one. I ran along, grabbing for the handrail that was on the outside of the car. I barely reached it and swung myself into the car. I looked back to see Donnie trip and fall along the side of the track.

"DONNIE!" I screamed. "GET UP!"

Donnie faded from sight as the train sped away into the darkness.

"Oh no!" I said out loud. "What else could go wrong?"

I looked around the inside of the boxcar, and although it was very dark, it was obvious that Jack's body was not in this car. I was close to the point of complete exhaustion and felt like crying.

What a mess we are in now, I thought. I've lost Jack, my bike, the wagon, and now Donnie. I sat down on the dirty floor of the boxcar and tried to catch my breath. I wrapped my arms around my legs and propped my forehead against my knees.

OK, pull yourself together. I can figure this out. When the train slows at the river crossing, I will hop out and run ahead to find Jack. I can pull him out myself, but how the heck am I gonna get him the rest of the way without Donnie?

C hapter 23

Digger ran as fast as his skinny legs would carry him and quickly slipped through the front gate. He was certain that he was being pursued by another vicious dog, and he made a hasty retreat to the safety of his cruiser. Sitting in the front seat, Digger lit a cigarette and tried to calm himself down. Try as he might, he could not figure out why Jack Feather's body was in the middle of Walker's Junk Yard.

"Something very squirrely is going on around here," thought Digger.

Digger started the patrol car and pulled away. He stopped in front of Lavonia's trailer, got out, and quickly jogged to the front porch, nervously watching over his shoulder as he went. He knocked on the trailer door and Lavonia appeared.

"Hi Digger," said Lavonia. "Did you speak to those boys?"

"Uh, no Mam. I looked all over back there and couldn't find any sign of them." Digger decided to lie.

"Are you sure they said they were back there?" Digger pointed toward the woods.

"I'm sure."

"Are you OK?" asked Lavonia. "You look like you saw a ghost."

"I'm fine," said Digger defensively.

"I appreciate you coming out here," said Lavonia. "You want to come in for a soft drink or something? I think I have some root beer left if Donnie and that other kid didn't drink them all."

"No thanks. I better be getting back to work." Digger turned to leave and did a double-take. "Did you say Donnie?"

"Yes, it was Donnie Green," answered Lavonia. "Didn't the Sheriff mention that?"

"No, he didn't say who they were. I don't think he knew."

"Well, maybe I didn't mention it. I thought I did."

"If they come by again, give the Sheriff a call."

"I'll do that. Good night, Digger."

"Good night." Digger got back in his patrol car and drove off. Why in the world was Jack's body in the middle of that junk yard? Was there some kind of ghoulish thing going on over there? Digger got the creeps every time he thought about Jack's face. And those lunatic dogs. What was that all about?

Digger was perplexed. *I should radio the Sheriff and tell him I found the body. But then I won't get any credit for my detective work. The only way I will impress Sheriff Langston is if I solve this case.* Unsure of what to do next, he decided to cruise around for a while and think about this situation.

Lavonia watched Digger as he drove away, then went back inside and sat down at the kitchen table. *I wish the Sheriff had come instead of Digger,* she thought. *That deputy doesn't have walking around sense and something about the way he was acting just didn't sit right.* She took the phone directory out of the pantry and looked up the number for Minzo Green.

I don't care if everybody is asleep over there, he needs to know that his son is wandering around town in the middle of the night, thought Lavonia as she dialed the number.

Chapter 24

At that moment, inside that dark, dirty boxcar, I was ready to give up and go home. Here I was, almost 14 years old, crying uncontrollably, and this was the second time in as many days that I had broken down like a little girl. I was too old to be crying. But once the tears began flowing, it was impossible to stop them. Donnie was right, this was a stupid, harebrained idea, and now I had no idea where he was or how I would get Jack to his house without Donnie's help. I even imagined I could hear harmonica notes. Wait a minute, I AM hearing a harmonica. I went to the open door and peered down the track. To my surprise, Donnie was hanging onto the outside of the car. I can't remember when I've ever been happier to see anyone.

"GET ME...TWEET...OFF THE...TWONK...SIDE OF THIS CAR...TWEET!" yelled Donnie between harmonica notes. He was perched precariously on a thin ledge that ran along the side of the car, holding onto a small handrail and still holding that darn harmonica in his mouth.

"TAKE MY HAND," I yelled and leaned as far out of the train car as I dared. The sound of the huge steel wheels spinning just below us was deafening. A slip here would mean the loss of a leg... or worse.

I ...TWEET...CAN'T!" yelled Donnie. "I'M ...TWONK ...AFRAID ...TWONK ... TO LET GO!"

Suddenly, a tree branch that overhung the track raked across my back and struck Donnie in the face.

"AHHHHHHHHHHH...TWEEEEEEEEEET" screamed Donnie. He was falling from the car when at the last possible instance, he lunged forward and grabbed my hand. I pulled him through the open door, and we both fell onto the floor of the car.

"I thought I was gonner die," said Donnie as we lay gasping on the dirty floor.

"Donnie, I have some bad news. I got no idea where Jack is. He definitely ain't in this car."

"That's brootiful! Let's prack up and go home then."

"You know we can't do that yet."

"I know," said Donnie dejectedly. "What are we gonner do then?"

"When the train slows down at the river crossing, we can run ahead to each car until we find him. We should have enough time to find him and get him off."

"I hope so," said Donnie.

Donnie and I rode in silence for about 30 minutes. Just before reaching the river, a heavy fog began to settle in, and the train began to slow down.

"We must be getting close to the river bridge," said Donnie. "We better get ready to jump off."

"I just hope we can find Jack."

After a few minutes more, the train slowed enough for us to easily jump off just before the river bridge. We ran ahead, looking in each car and quickly found Jack. We pulled him off onto the siding and carried him down the grade to the riverbank. The river was now shrouded in a heavy fog.

"Dang, we messed up again!" said Donnie. "Jack's house is on the other side of the river. We should have stayed on the train and jumped off on the other side. We have to figure out a way to get him across."

"We could carry him across the river bridge, but that would be hard to do. It's hard enough just walking that railroad trestle, much less trying to carry a body across one."

Donnie sat down on the riverbank and began playing "Old Man River" on his harmonica.

"Donnie, give me the flashlight. I'll check that bridge out. Maybe it won't be so hard to get Jack across." I switched on the light and started to walk back up to the train tracks when I spotted something on the riverbank just upstream. The light shone upon a small boat that was pulled up underneath the railroad bridge.

"Donnie, look! A boat!" I walked to the base of the bridge and inspected the small craft. "It looks pretty good. We can load up Jack, and the three of us can float the rest of the way to his house. Jack's place is not too far below the railroad bridge. We should be there in just a few minutes."

"Let's get Jack in the boat and get this over with," said Donnie. "I am so exhausted that I can barely keep my eyes open."

We carried Jack over to the boat and loaded him in. That's when Donnie noticed the wood that the boat was constructed from.

"Son of a gun. This boat is made out of cedar. You can see the red and white wood. Jack said that cedar was special to the Cherokee."

"You can smell it too," I added. "Maybe this means that our luck is about to change."

"I hope you're right, because it couldn't get much worse."

C hapter 25

Minzo got out of bed and staggered to the kitchen. He had ignored the ringing as long as he could, hoping whoever was calling would
give up. Must be another car crash out on the highway, he thought. I
hope it's not another carload of kids. Those accidents just tore him to
pieces for weeks afterwards. Minzo lifted the receiver from its cradle.

"Hello."

"Mr. Green, this is Lavonia Monet. I'm sorry to bother you at this
hour, but are you aware that Donnie is out wandering around at this
hour of the night?"

"What?" said Minzo. "Lavonia, you must be mistaken because Donnie is in his bed right now."

"Are you sure about that? Because he was just at my place about half
an hour ago with that Dodge boy."

"Hold on just a minute."

Minzo walked to the rear of the house and pushed the door open to
the boy's bedroom. He pulled the covers back on Donnie's bed to find
a wadded-up jacket and some dirty clothes where Donnie should have
been.

"Son-of-a...!!" said Minzo in disgust.

He walked back to the kitchen.

"Lavonia, I just checked his room, and he's snuck out somewhere
again. What did he say when you saw him?"

"They said they was camping out at Fat Man's Squeeze. They came
to the trailer to get a drink of water and was acting kind of strange, so
I thought something was going on. I called Sheriff Langston as soon as
they left, and he sent Digger over here. He looked around and said he
didn't see them anywhere. I figured I'd better call you to let you know."

"This is not the first time he has pulled something like this. I appreciate you calling."

"I'm gonna whip that boy's butt," said Minzo out loud as he dialed the Sheriff's House. The phone rang only a few times before Sheriff Langston answered.

"Sheriff Langston."

"Hi Jeff, this is Minzo. Lavonia just called me and said she saw Donnie and Rick Dodge over at her place a little while ago."

"Yeah, I know," said Jeff. "She called me, too. I sent Digger over there to check it out, but I haven't heard back from him. I didn't want to worry you, but they shouldn't be wandering around like that."

"Donnie snuck out of the house," said Minzo. "He didn't tell anyone about camping out."

"Well, if him and that Dodge boy are together, there is no telling what is going on," said the Sheriff. "I'll try to raise Digger on the radio and see what he found out. I'll head over to Lavonia's as soon as I get my clothes on and see if I can find them. I'm afraid Digger couldn't find his butt with both hands. I'll give you a call as soon as I find out something."

"You don't have to call because I'm going over there myself. I'll see you there in a few minutes."

"O.K. see you there." Sheriff Langston hung up and reached for the police radio microphone.

"Digger, have you got your ears on?"

The sound of the Sheriff's voice over the radio broke the silence and startled Digger. He fumbled for the microphone while trying to keep the cruiser on the highway.

"This is Deputy Phelps. Over."

"Digger, did you locate those boys? Over"

"I looked all around and didn't find them. Maybe they went home. Over."

"I don't think so. Minzo just called and said that Donnie snuck out of the house. I suspect that Rick's parents don't know he is out, also. My guess is those boys are up to something. I'm gonna meet Minzo at Lavonia's in about 20 minutes. I want you over there as well. Over"

“Ten-four. I’ll see you there. Over”
“Over and out.”

Chapter 26

Getting Jack into the small boat was no problem. But we had no way of paddling the boat, so Donnie and I searched up and down the riverbank until we found an old board that would work reasonably well. We shoved the boat out into the Warrior. Fortunately, the current was with us, and all we had to do was paddle to the opposite bank and drift about a quarter mile downstream to Jack's house. The only problem was the thick fog that had settled into the river valley.

"I can't see squat," said Donnie as he paddled the boat toward the opposite bank. "I hope we're heading in the right direction."

"If we just keep moving across this current, we have to hit the other bank."

Suddenly, something thumped against the side of the boat.

"What was that?" asked Donnie. He pulled the flashlight from his pocket and shone it across the brown waters of the Warrior.

"Look at that!" said Donnie in disbelief.

The surface of the river was alive with swirling fish. They were jumping all around the boat as far as we could see in every direction. One had hit the side of the boat another one jumped clear over the side into the boat.

"This is really creepy," I said. "It's just like when Jack and I were fishing that day. It's like the fish know that Jack is in this boat. They must know that we are taking him home."

"You're creeping me out again, Rick."

"Do you have a better explanation?"

Donnie tossed the hapless fish overboard, and another one immediately jumped into the boat.

"Strupid fish," said Donnie as he pitched the other one out again.

The fish coalesced into a huge school and began slowly circling the boat.

"This is definitely weird," I said. "Listen, do you hear that?"

A low rumbling sound seemed to be coming from all around us.

"I hear it. Are the fish making that sound?"

"I never heard fish sound like that. It must be another train crossing the river bridge."

"That don't sound like no train," said Donnie.

The sound was now much louder, and it seemed to be coming from up river. The fish continued circling the boat.

"Oh no, it's a tug boat. Donnie, paddle harder, we gotta get off this river."

"I'm about spent, you paddle a while." Donnie handed me the board.

I began furiously paddling but had no idea which way I was going. Suddenly, the fog parted, and the moon shone with an intensity I had never seen before. The area around us was illuminated by an intense white light.

"What the heck!" said Donnie, surprised.

We both turned in the direction of the light to see the gigantic bow of a boat bearing down on us from out of the fog.

"PADDLE, PADDLE," screamed Donnie.

The last thing I remember was the sound of breaking wood and then the cold river water. I was drawn down into the blackness. It felt as if my lungs would burst. The urge to inhale was overpowering, and I knew I would very soon lose consciousness. Suddenly, I saw Jack standing on the riverbank smiling, his arms outstretched as if beckoning. Jack spoke in Cherokee, but I understood every word.

"Rick," he said. "Your journey isn't over yet........ You promised....... You promised!"

I reached out to take his hand, but couldn't grasp it. I swam toward him, and when I thought I could swim no more, I broke through the surface of the water, gasping for air. By chance, a piece of the boat was there, and I clung to it. The current continued to take me downriver, and I kicked the wreckage in the direction that I hoped was the riverbank. Feeling the river bottom against my bare feet, I waded to shore and fell onto the muddy bank. I didn't know if I would ever get up again.

Chapter 27

Minzo arrived at Lavonia's trailer to find Sheriff Langston and Deputy Phelps having a heated conversation in the front yard. Sheriff Langston was visibly upset and was giving Digger a good tongue-lashing.

"And when exactly did you discover the break-in at the Coroner's Office, Digger?"

"I guess it was about 12:00 or so," said Digger dejectedly.

"Digger, that was 5 hours ago, and when exactly were you going to report this?"

"I thought I could solve the case myself. I did find the body."

"What body are we talking about?" asked Minzo as he walked up.

"Minzo, Digger says there was a break-in at your office about midnight tonight," said Sheriff Langston.

"What?" said Minzo, obviously perturbed. "Who would want to break into the Coroner's Office? Was anything taken?"

"We don't know who did it, but they took Jack Feather," said Digger. "I found his body over in Walker's Junk Yard.

"Hold on! You mean Jack Feather's body is in Walker's? This is the craziest thing I have ever heard. Are you sure about all of this?"

"Yes, sir," said Digger. "But we just checked the junk yard and it ain't there no more."

"Jeff, did you ask Lavonia about Donnie and Rick?" asked Minzo.

"I just spoke with her," said Sheriff Langston. "She said they came to her trailer about two hours ago and asked for some water and then left."

"Wait a minute!" exclaimed Minzo. "I think I just figured this out. Do you remember that Donnie asked me about seeing that Jack got buried at his house?"

"I think I remember you saying something about that," said Sheriff Langston. "Didn't you tell him that it should be no problem?"

"Unfortunately, I did tell him that. I see now that it was a mistake."

"Do you think Donnie sneaking out of the house has something to do with the break-in?"

"I suspect those boys are very much involved in this," said Minzo. We'd better give Tom Dodge a call and see if his son's home. If he's also missing, then I know exactly where they are heading."

C hapter 28
How long I lay on the side of the river trying to recover, I have no idea. I was shivering so hard that I thought my bones would break. My first thought was to try to locate Donnie. I prayed that he was OK, but I was not optimistic. As I was about to start searching, I heard a voice calling from just upriver.

"HELLO!"

It's Donnie, I thought. Thank goodness he's alive.

"DONNIE!" I yelled. "WHERE ARE YOU?" I drug myself in the direction of the voice. "ARE YOU OK?" I came upon a stranger bent over a body on the side of the river.

"I'm afraid your buddy didn't make it," said the tall fellow.

"Oh, heaven help me! This is all my fault. Donnie, I'm so sorry. I should have never talked him into this."

"Son, there wasn't much anyone could have done," said the stranger. "I pulled him out of the river as soon as I saw you go down. I guess he was just too old to be trying to swim in that cold water. I suspect he might have had a heart attack."

"Too old?" I asked. It was at that point I realized that this fellow had pulled Jack's body from the river. It wasn't Donnie after all.

"Son, my name is Tom Wells, and I'm the captain of the Crimson Tide tug boat. What in the world were you doing in the middle of the river at this time of night?" asked Tom.

"It's a long story."

"Well, I've gotta try to locate the Tide. She's adrift in the river and probably run aground somewhere, or worse. Will you be OK if I leave you here for a while? There's an old house right up the bank there. I'm gonna find my tug, and then I can radio for someone to come get you."

"There's a house right up the bank there?" I asked.

"Just up there," said Tom, pointing up the bank. "You can't miss it. Maybe they've got a phone that we could use."

By chance, we were not 100 feet from Jack's old house.

"I'll be fine if you need to go. But could you help me carry Jack up to that house?" I asked. "Right now, I'm not sure I could get myself up there."

"No problem," said Tom as he picked up Jack. Tom carried Jack up to the house and placed him on the front porch. Walking the few feet to the house required all the effort I could muster. I was thankful that Captain Tom was there.

"It looks like no one is home. You wait here, and I'll go down to the fishing camp. It's about a mile downriver. Will you be OK here?"

"Yes, sir, I'll be fine."

Tom took off at a trot down the river road.

C hapter 29
I was quickly approaching a state of complete exhaustion, both physical and mental. Dragging Jack around to the back of the house to his final resting place was the hardest thing I had ever done in my entire life. It took all the strength I had left to cover the short distance. When I finally got him situated in his grave, I collapsed on top of the pile of earth next to the hole. I lay there for a few minutes to catch my breath and then, without getting up, used my feet to slowly push earth in on top of Jack. Fortunately, the fog lifted somewhat, and the moon shone through the tree tops. The light revealed a shovel propped against Jack's house, which I used to finish filling in the hole. I then began moving the pile of stones that Jack told us to place on the grave site. My arms were so tired that I had to drag each stone across the ground to place it on the pile. I tossed aside an old mason jar that was buried there and finished placing the last of the stones, arranging them into a crude grave marker. Sitting down on the ground next to Jack's grave and with my head in my hands, I began weeping. Despite the fatigue and overwhelming sadness, I knew my job was not yet over. I knelt in the muddy earth beside Jack's grave.

"Dear Lord. Please take care of Jack Feather." Tears began streaming down my face again, but I just let them flow. "He had a tough life, and now he is on his way to Heaven. He said he wants to come back as a mountain lion or an eagle or something like that, and if you could make that happen, I know he would appreciate it. If you could make him come back as a dog, then it would be OK with me if it was a terrier that could tree squirrels. But that's up to you, of course. Also, my friend Donnie might be on his way up to you, too. He's a good guy and was my best friend of all time. I know he has done a lot of stupid things, but don't be too hard on him........"

"What the heck do you mean, I've done a lot of sturpid things?" demanded Donnie as he came around the corner of Jack's house. "The only sturpid things I've done is let you talk me into doing crazy sturff like this."

"DONNIE!!!!!" I rushed up to him and threw my arms around him. I was crying like a little girl. "I can't believe it. You're not drowned!"

"Hey! You don't have to get all brubbery!" said Donnie as he pushed me away.

"What happened to you?"

"Well, when that old trug boat hit us, I went down pretty deep and thought it was all over. You're gronna think I'm crazy, but I swear to you, Jack was calling to me. He was an angel, and he saved my life."

Goose-bumps formed all over my body, and the hair stood up on the back of my neck.

"That is exactly what happened to me! Jack told me to swim toward him, and that's what saved my life. Man is that weird, or what?!!"

"I came ashore on the other side of the river," said Donnie, "and after searching around a while, I walked back up to the river bridge and crossed over to this side. I hoped you might be over here."

Suddenly, headlights flashed across the forest as three cars skidded to a halt in front of Jack's house. I recognized each: the Coroner's, the Sheriff's, and my dad's. Although I knew that we were in serious trouble, a wave of relief came over me. It was finally over.

Donnie and I walked around to the front of the house to find Sheriff Langston, Deputy Phelps, Minzo, and Dad looking very perturbed.

"Donnie, what in the heck have you boys done?" asked Minzo. "Everyone has been worried sick. Your Mom is fit to be tied. What have you got to say for yourself?"

Dad, looking very angry, took me by the arm. "Rick, what in the world is going on?"

"This is all my fault, Dad. I made Donnie help me."

"Wait just a minute," said Donnie. "This is as much my fault as it is Rick's."

"Donnie, let Rick finish," said Dad. "Rick, you'd better start explaining and fast. There have been laws broken. This is serious stuff."

"I apologize to everyone," I said. "When I heard that Jack was gonna be buried in Montgomery, I knew I couldn't let that happen. Last summer, before Jack died, we promised that we would make sure he was buried on his property, and I was gonna do that no matter what."

"You boys carried Jack all the way from Minzo's office to bury him here?" asked Dad. "That's over 10 miles."

"Yes, sir," I said. "We kind of accidentally broke the window at Uncle Minzo's office. We didn't do anything else except take Jack."

"And he's buried here?" asked Minzo.

"Yes, sir. The tug boat captain helped me carry him up from the river bank and..."

"Tug boat Captain?" Dad asked. "What are you talking about?"

"Well after we hopped that train, we kind of got ran over by a trug boat out in the river." said Donnie.

"WHAT!" said Minzo. "Stealing bodies, breaking in, hopping trains, tug boats. Are you boys crazy?"

"Minzo, calm down," said Sheriff Langston. "My idiot deputy knew about that break-in 5 hours ago. If he had reported it, we might have prevented this whole thing."

"Thank God no one was hurt," said Dad. "Rick, you will be paying for any damage you have done, and you're gonna apologize to everyone for all the trouble you caused."

"Yes, sir," I said as I gazed at my bare feet, not wanting to make eye contact with anyone.

Sheriff Langston and Digger walked around to the back of the house to examine the grave site. A pile of stones marked the grave. An old mason jar near the grave site caught the Sheriff's eye. He picked it up and noticed that it was sealed and contained a bundle of papers.

"That's odd," said the Sheriff to Digger. "There's writing on these papers."

Their flashlight beams preceded them as they returned from their investigation. They found everyone involved in a heated conversation in the front yard.

"We'll just have to dig Jack up and deliver him to the state for proper burial," said Minzo.

"NO!" I demanded. "Dad, you can't let them do that. Didn't you teach me that I should always keep my promises, and Mr. Green, you told Donnie that Jack could be buried on his property. Didn't you say that?"

"Well, yes, I said that, but this property no longer belongs to Jack. The state of Alabama will sell it at auction, and believe me, a grave is not gonna be allowed here."

Sheriff Langston was paying no attention to the conversation as he used his flashlight to read the papers that he had removed from the jar.

"Minzo," said Sheriff Langston, "I don't think there is gonna be a problem with having Jack buried here."

"What are you talking about, Jeff?" asked Minzo. "We've already had this conversation."

"I just found some papers in a Mason jar back there," said the Sheriff.

"That old jar was buried in those stones that Jack piled up for his grave marker," I said.

"These papers are the *Last Will and Testament* of Mr. Jack Feather," said the Sheriff, holding the papers up for everyone to see.

All arguing stopped at that announcement.

"Jack must have known that he was dying. He purposely planted these papers knowing that Rick would find them," said the Sheriff. "Let me read what it says here."

"I, Jack Feather, being of sound mind and body, leave this house and the surrounding 100 acres of land to Mr. Richard Dodge," read the Sheriff.

"I don't know the law completely in these matters but this document is notarized, and I'm pretty sure Rick has the right to bury Jack on his own property."

No one knew what to say, but Donnie summed it up nicely......"Brootiful!"

"I guess this is yours also, Rick," said Sheriff Langston as he dropped a silver dollar in my hand.

E PILOGUE

A few days later, with the help of the *Echota Cherokee Tribe of Alabama*, Jack Feather received a proper burial with a full ceremony. His final resting place would be the land where, I want to believe, he had spent some of the best years of his life. Afterwards, needing time to myself, Dad said I could walk back home. With a fiery sun setting in a cloudless blue sky, I pulled off my shoes and headed home. The forest along the Warrior was unusually quiet, no crickets, no frogs singing, just the low, soft hiss of wind in trees and the fall of my bare feet along the river trail. The cool air overlying the warm river water spawned a thin mist that clung to my skin and clothing. Turning a bend in the river, I stopped as I heard a rustling just ahead in the trail. The fog parted momentarily to reveal a snow-white panther standing in the trail ahead. By all rights, I should have been petrified, but I felt no fear at all. The big cat looked straight at me, turned, and silently stole away into the night. It was at that moment that I knew another Cherokee brave had found his place in the cosmos.

ACKNOWLEDGMENTS

I wish to thank my wife, Cheryl, for constructive reviews of the manuscript, my son TJ for providing the 15-year-old perspective, and my daughter Erin for her help. Ms. Sydney Nelson provided helpful comments. I am grateful for the assistance of Dr. Ed Keiser. Dr. Luther Knight provided many helpful suggestions, and to him I am very grateful. Finally, Dr. Paul Lago gave the manuscript a thorough review and provided helpful suggestions and I am very appreciative of his help.

www.ingramcontent.com/pod-product-compliance
Lightning Source LLC
Chambersburg PA
CBHW071533100726
47908CB00004B/1386